An Inferno of Ire

Kristen King

Contents

Jo's Strawberry Lemonade For Delight

For the simple syrup:

1 cup sugar

4 cups water

For fruit blend:

2 cups fresh strawberries

1 cup lemon juice, or 3-4 lemons

2 cups water

Additions:

3 cups ice
Sliced strawberries for decoration
Sprig of basil leaves

Combine sugar and water in a saucepan over medium heat. Stir with a wooden spoon while chanting,

Earth, air, fire, and water, infuse this syrup with delight for the hour.

Once the sugar dissolves, set aside to cool.

Blend the strawberries with the lemon juice and water until smooth. Add the simple syrup to the blender. As you blend for just a few seconds until mixed, say aloud,

Summon the sweetness. Summon the tart. Bring them together for a marvelous jumpstart.

Strain through a metal sieve to remove any seeds.

Add sliced strawberries and 3 cups of ice to a large pitcher. Pour the strawberry mixture over the ice, top with a sprig of basil, and enjoy!

Chapter 1

The scent of smoldering holy basil wafted from a small cast iron pot on the hearth room table at Parchment and Pine. Autumn blew a breath into both of her palms and snuffed out any remaining sparks of her growing fire magic. As the two other witches and her friend Anabeth eyed her, she paced around the room, contemplating. Her orange tabby cat familiar, Tavish, brushed up against her leg for support.

Autumn held out a hand as Anabeth offered her phone and swallowed deeply with distress. Staring at the image on the screen, Autumn noted wrinkled graph paper and old symbols scribbled into formulas on it. She exchanged a glance with her cousin Simone before focusing on Anabeth and Finn, who had just come in with news of a fire at the university laboratory.

"Let's start with the basics on this one. Something tells me we need to know more about your cousin, Rowan, before we dive into this as an arson and . . . ultimately, a murder." Autumn met eyes with Anabeth, who tried to hold it together long enough for their conversation.

Anabeth batted away tears forming in her eyes and looked toward the blazing fire in the hearth for a moment. "Rowan had an apartment near the university. I have a key, so we can head over there whenever you're ready. I can show you some of her things, and maybe that'll give you some information about her."

"The police haven't cordoned off her apartment?" Simone interjected with directness as usual.

Shaking her head, Anabeth considered it for a moment. "I don't think so. They're more concerned with the university lab and seeing the lab fire as an accident. I'm pretty sure they're still determining whether or not it was really arson, but there's no way it was just an accident. Rowan knew something was going on in there, and it's just too much to be a coincidence. If being a journalist has taught me anything, it's that there's always more to the story."

Finn took a step forward, away from the hearth, and nodded to his mentor, Anabeth. "Since I'll be covering the story, instead of Anabeth, I'll keep my eyes and ears open and let you all know if they uncover more."

"Thanks, Finn." Autumn smiled at him as she received a download in her mind. "And it may be a good idea if you pay attention to how the fire started. You know, like what activated it or fueled it. Plus, we need to know if someone targeted Rowan specifically."

Grabbing a notepad from his back pants pocket, Finn nodded in agreement. "Gotcha. I'll poke my nose around and see what I can find out."

"Oh, and you knew these symbols came from ancient alchemy. How did you know that?" Autumn lifted Anabeth's phone and showed the image to Finn.

Finn laughed under his breath and glanced between the other two elemental witches in the room. "My aunt, Rose Carmichael, taught me a thing or two when I was younger. I spent a few summers in Hollow's Glenn at her house. She likes to dabble in alchemy, being a doctor and all. I think chemistry was one of her favorite subjects in school."

"Interesting." Simone lifted an eyebrow and looked at her cousin. "I bet your mom knows a bit about Dr. Carmichael's dabbling, Autumn. They've been pretty good friends over the years, haven't they?"

Autumn nodded at Simone. "Yeah, they have. If we approached the two of them, then they'd be able to point us in the right direction to start. We've gotta find out more about these symbols. All I can pick out here are the triangles for earth and fire."

"Those are the basics, but you have to combine them to actually transmute energy." Finn cocked his head to one side and paused. "I mean, I'm sure you have firsthand knowledge of changing energy and all."

Simone laughed. "What would give you that impression?"

Shoving his hands into his jeans pockets, Finn shrugged and tipped back and forth on his heels and toes. "Well, I may be new in town, but I know a thing or two about Autumn, the new four-points witch, and her coven."

"Geez! News travels fast around here!" Simone looked wide-eyed at Autumn.

"Autumn, I'm just a regular person." Anabeth smiled softly. "And since even I've seen what you can do, there's no doubt all the witches in the region know who you are by now."

"I see." Autumn pursed her lips and looked down at Tavish at her feet. "I thought only the founding families knew about my growing gifts. Apparently it's the entire region."

"Well"—Anabeth stood up and threw her bag over her shoulder—"I'm sure most people are still living their normal lives unaware that this whole witch underground exists, but Finn is right. Every witch within a hundred-mile radius must know you can change energy at your will. Unless they've been living under a rock for the past few months."

"Wow, you're famous." Simone smirked and crossed her arms.

Autumn covered her eyes with her hands for a moment and shook her head. "Thanks, Sim. That's just what I wanted.

We're supposed to be quietly keeping the energy balance of the region, not putting ourselves on stage."

"If it helps any, I think this could actually be a good thing." Finn grabbed his own messenger bag and started following Anabeth toward the hearth room curtains. "If your coven is serious about maintaining the balance, then what better way to do it? People know to come to you when they're in a tough spot. You're like the modern-day witch versions of Sherlock and Watson. Honestly, why do you think we came here first?"

"He's right, Autumn." Simone nodded in agreement while opening the curtains to the hearth room. "It's the reason Sorcha came to us with her sister's disappearance and why James always comes to us with his dreams. And sidenote, he's bound to be stopping by with another one soon since this recent case came on the radar."

Autumn walked beside Anabeth as they all wandered through the shop. "I guess I see how it's a good thing people come to us, but I don't want to draw unnecessary attention to all the elemental witches. Blending in keeps the balance protected." She paused and felt a strong pull toward a black tourmaline pendulum hanging from a new display on the center table.

"What is it?" Anabeth questioned as Autumn stood eyeing the table.

Picking up the pendulum, Autumn held it at eye level to receive some insight. She smiled and grabbed for Anabeth's hand. "This needs to go home with you. It's a black tourmaline crystal. Hang it up on your front door to protect you and the energy inside." Autumn dropped the pendulum into Anabeth's hand and closed her fingers around it.

"Oh, okay. Let me pay you for it, then." Anabeth scrambled to open her bag, but Autumn shook her head.

"No, don't worry about it. You're meant to have it. Plus . . ." Anabeth walked over to the side wall and grabbed a small kraft paper bag off a tall wooden hutch. She spun around to hand the little bag to Anabeth. "Juniper berry tea. Drink it twice a day for protection."

Anabeth sighed. "Autumn, why do I need all of this? I'm not the one in trouble. My cousin, Rowan, was." A lump formed in her throat as she thought about Rowan's last moments in the burning laboratory.

Autumn grabbed Anabeth's shoulders and looked her square in the eyes. "There's something going on beyond what we see. You know that. I don't want you getting hurt because of all this, and I just know that you need these right now, okay? So just take them and humor me."

"She's never wrong, Anabeth. Just go with it," Simone called from the back of the shop.

"All right, better safe than sorry." Anabeth smiled and headed toward the door. "Thank you both for helping. I feel better knowing you're looking into Rowan's death and this fire as well."

"We're gonna do everything we can to help." Autumn opened the front door for Anabeth and Finn. "We'll let you know what we find out, okay? And Finn, let your aunt know to expect a call from my mother."

"Yep, I'm on it. And I'll keep you posted about what I find as well." Finn pulled his messenger bag strap up higher on his shoulder as he walked onto the sidewalk with Anabeth. "Off to dive into more local stories."

Anabeth gave a tight-lipped smile and nodded as she walked outside with Finn. Autumn watched the two of them start down a color-dotted Main Street lined with brilliant red, yellow, and white flowers for summer. As they continued, she glimpsed golden shimmers dancing around Finn's back pocket where he kept his notebook. She couldn't help thinking to herself how he must be a pretty clever air witch himself.

Smiling at the thought, Autumn headed back into the shop while Tavish trotted the other way to the door again. She felt a pang of cherry cordial sweep over her before she could question the cat. Immediately, a smile came over her face as James walked through the door behind her.

"Hello, stranger," James said as Autumn turned and looked up into his warm brown eyes. He stroked her hair and kissed her lips softly.

"Mmm, that comforting energy of yours sure does have good timing." Autumn grabbed his hand and pulled him back into the shop as Tavish rubbed up against his leg.

"Good timing for what?" He looked at her curiously and then waved to Simone behind the counter.

"For keeping me grounded as we figure out the latest death, or possibly murder." Autumn patted one of the stools at the back counter, giving him the cue to sit. She took the one beside it and breathed in his scent of cherry cordial and chestnuts once more. "But you've got your own dream to share today, don't you?"

James sighed and looked between Autumn and Simone, who peered up from behind the computer with an I-told-you-so look. "Afraid so." He rubbed the back of his neck with his hand. "And this one isn't like any dream I've had before."

Chapter 2

Simone cleared her throat and stood up from behind the computer at Parchment and Pine. "Well, I called James having another one of his dreams from a mile away." She pulled her black T-shirt down around her waist and walked around the counter to put her hands on Autumn's and James's shoulders. "Why don't you two get some lunch and talk for a while? I'll hold down the fort here at the shop, and you can bring me back something to eat."

James tilted his head in Autumn's direction. "I have some sandwiches in the truck for a picnic lunch. Join me?"

Autumn smiled and turned to her cousin. "Sim, are you sure? I don't wanna leave as it gets busy."

Simone swiped her hand through the air. "Don't worry about me. I'm good here. Besides, you need to get the details of this new dream and spend some time together before things get out of control again. I'm sensing another wave of crazy energy coming our way." She headed toward the center of the store to spruce up one of the displays. "Just fill me in on the details of that dream when you get back, okay? And bring me this week's special iced tea from the Forest Brew."

Laughing while grabbing her brown vegan leather backpack at the front door, Autumn agreed. "You got it. And I'll grab a salad for you as well. Thanks for looking after the shop." She paused and eyed the displays while receiving a downloaded message. "Oh, you might want to put a couple of those new tissue paper suncatchers aside for Marion Bennett. I think she may wander in here at some point, and something tells me I should stay on her good side."

"Ah, there's my claircognizant cousin at work." Simone grabbed a couple suncatchers and moved them to a more prominent position on the display. "I'll make sure to show them to her."

"Thanks for giving us some time, Simone." James put his hand on Autumn's back to lead her out the front door. "We'll be back soon."

Simone shooed him out with her hand. "Yeah, yeah. Just spill the tea on that dream of yours."

"Got it. See you in a bit," he called as he gave Tavish a chin scratch before heading out the front.

James pulled his black truck door open for Autumn to climb in, and they made their way over to Hawthorn Cottage, the home the girls had inherited from their deceased grandmother.

Autumn walked up onto the front porch and grabbed a flannel blanket from one of the wooden chairs. "Come on, the woods are calling and there's a cozy spot in the clearing."

He took her hand and smiled as he lifted his cooler full of food from the ground. "Sounds good. You lead the way, and I'll start talking."

With each step down the path into the woods she considered her sanctuary, Autumn felt the deep connection to the earth beneath her. It welcomed home to this land as golden shimmers rose to meet her and encircled her feet just as Tavish did when he was excited to see her. The trees lining the path bent in the wind for them as they made their way further toward the clearing.

"So this latest dream," James started, "it felt almost surreal. Like a dream within a dream."

Autumn looked at him curiously as she glided over tree roots and branches with ease. "You have lucid dreams all the time and know that you're dreaming."

"Yes, but this felt different. I knew the dream was a premonition as it unfolded, and yet I also knew within the dream that it would never be real. I know that makes little sense, but that's what it felt like." He stepped over a few branches, trying to keep up with Autumn, who had no trouble negotiating the path.

Autumn stopped abruptly and turned to face him. Looking up to see his distraught face, she placed her hand on his temple. "Release the burden," she whispered under her breath.

A cooling breeze swept through the surrounding air, and his head felt instant relief from the stress of the dream. He placed his hand on top of hers and closed his eyes, focusing on the cooling sensation on his temple.

With a sigh, James opened his eyes and nodded. "Let's go sit down, and I'll tell you the rest."

Motioning to the clearing, Autumn took a few steps as a Steller's jay landed on a log in front of them. "Looks like that's our spot." She smiled and placed the flannel blanket down on the ground beside the log as the jay flew away.

James unpacked the sandwiches, watermelon slices, and lemonades from his cooler before sitting beside Autumn. "I know these woods have always been your sanctuary, but I'd like to think that they were mine as a child as well."

"Of course they're yours as well. That Steller's jay told me to welcome you back." Autumn grabbed a lemonade from him and continued. "Now, about that dream within a dream. Tell me what you saw."

James sighed and took a swig of his lemonade. "An older woman in dark-purple robes. She walked within the shadows of the trees in a thick forest that looked somewhat burned. I saw her just beyond a bubbling cauldron with some kind of smoke billowing from it. And the smell . . . I remember an intense sulfur around me." He ran a hand over his face and continued. "The woman in robes beckoned me forward, but as I moved closer, she shapeshifted before my eyes."

Autumn squinted at her sandwich and thought for a moment. "So not only did you have the vision of the dream, but you also experienced the sulfur smell." She paused and put a hand on his arm. "And this woman . . . James, I've never known a real shapeshifter. That's the stuff of myths and legends. Do you think that's why it seemed surreal?"

He shook his head at her as he chomped on a piece of watermelon. "The whole thing felt surreal. I watched this scene play out in the dream while feeling like it was all an illusion. Yet, in all my other dreams, I'm actually living out what will happen in the future, and I know it's a premonition. This one came to me almost as a fantasy story played out before me."

"Okay, so let's try to make some sense of it. We have this strange older woman in dark robes walking around in the forest. Plus, there's the cauldron brewing." Autumn looked through the trees surrounding them. "What would someone be doing as they wandered the forest?"

"Maybe you should ask yourself that question." He laughed at her as she appeared deep in thought.

Autumn gave him a nudge, and James leaned in to give her a kiss. "I'm just saying that you're the one who comes into the woods to lose yourself . . . or maybe regain your sense of self."

"Yeah, it's about the connection to the elements for me here in the woods. And you mentioned that the forest looked almost burned in your dream. Not to mention that a cauldron bubbled away with smoke pouring from it." Autumn bit into her watermelon and closed her eyes. "More fire energy at play, but why?"

"It is summer. Maybe it's telling us a time frame for something to occur." He shrugged and felt another cool breeze shift across the clearing, sending Autumn's long auburn hair flying gently into his face. He brushed it behind her shoulder as she opened her eyes.

The breeze sparked a thought in her. "The fire of summer matched with the earth of the woods and smoke carried by air."

"Oh man, I don't like where you're going with this. Every time the elements converge, there's some kind of disaster."

She put her hand on his forearm and shook her head. "This doesn't feel quite like that, but something pulls at me from all four directions as you describe the dream. I keep thinking about the intensity of the fire, though, and my thoughts come back to the burned woods." She looked at him with seriousness in her eyes. "This latest death that Anabeth asked us to help with . . . it happened in a fire at the university chemistry lab."

James sighed with worry. "Autumn, why didn't you tell me before?"

"I didn't know how it might relate to your dream, but now that you've told me the details, it's pretty clear we're dealing with fire here."

"And you're still developing your fire energy." James wrapped his arm around her and pulled her close.

"I'm getting better with it every day, but yeah. I need to find Lainy and let her know the coven needs her gifts this time around." Autumn entangled her fingers in his. "James, this next month may pull me in lots of different directions. I need some time to connect with my father and the ancestors and to sort this all out."

He tucked his face into her hair and took a deep breath, recalling the words the palm reader had said to him several months back. Autumn would need time to herself, and her family needed her above all else.

"I know." James tightly squeezed her against his chest. "You need the space to learn who you really are."

She turned and brushed her hand gently across his face. "I know my father will return soon, and I should be prepared to see him and learn about that part of myself. Not to mention, this case might push my fire magic beyond its current capability. I need to work with Lainy and keep honing my skills." She gave him an apologetic look and pressed her hands flat against his chest, pushing him down to the ground. Hovering over him, she locked eyes with him. "Don't think for a second that this means I'm letting you go, though, because we're only getting started."

Laughing, he brought her wrist up toward his face and brushed over it with his thumb. A faint shimmer revealed what he had seen once before: an outstretched owl with a Celtic quaternary knot in its claws on the surface of her skin. As he kissed the shimmering emblem, it disappeared once again. "I'll wait as long as it takes for the owl watching over my dreams."

"I know." She kissed him and whispered, "I'll wait for you, too."

"Just remember our promise." He lifted her chin to raise her eyes to his. "You'll let me watch over you, too."

Chapter 3

Autumn threw her coat over the hooks under the stairs at Crescent House, Aunt Jo's home. The wafting smells of roasted corn and asparagus swam through the hallway toward the girls' noses.

"Hey, thanks for watching the shop at lunch today. I appreciated seeing James for a while and getting into the woods." Autumn smiled at Simone and picked up Tavish from under her feet.

"Oh, you went into the woods, did you?" Simone gave her cousin a sideways smile. "So that thing you said about needing some space only lasted about a day, huh?"

Autumn swatted her hand at Simone as they walked into the kitchen. "Would you stop? I told you. I want to see him, and I know we have a future together. It's just that now isn't the time to really develop things."

"If you say so." Simone eyed her cousin curiously, wondering what this was truly about.

"Oh, hello, dears!" Jo called as she dropped a wooden spoon beside the stove and came over to give them both hugs. "Just you two this evening? I thought Lainy planned to come for dinner as well."

"She's taking a martial arts class over at the community center." Simone found a piece of pita bread and scooped it into a bowl of hummus on the kitchen counter. "I think she's hooked."

"Well, it's lovely that she's getting active in the community. How was the day for you both?" She paused for a moment as her intuition set in. "No, not again!"

"What's the matter, Josephine?" Penny wandered through the back door carrying a large wicker basket full of lavender and chamomile flowers. "I heard you yell in the backyard!"

Penny looked at her sister and then at the girls. Staring at Autumn, she knew just as Jo had that something was the matter. "More bad news? Really?"

Jo sighed and took the basket from her sister. "Honestly, we find out Autumn's the new four-points witch, and the whole mountain region goes crazy!" She threw one hand up as the other set the flowers onto the large kitchen island. The two older women began sorting the long stems into bundles. "Well, let's hear it before we're very much older. Poison, kidnapping, or black magic? Which needs to be dealt with today?"

Chuckling at her sister, Penny pulled a large spool of brown twine and scissors from a kitchen drawer. She wrapped each of the flower bundles with the twine and strung them up over the kitchen sink window.

"You're feeling awfully dramatic today, Mom. What's gotten into you?" Simone headed for the oven as a timer went off, and she pulled out a large baking tray with an asparagus and gruyere tart browning atop it. "I mean, whatever makes you cook like this, I'll take it."

"I'm just antsy for the coming summer solstice. Don't mind me." Jo peered over Simone's shoulder to eye the tart. "Perfect." She wiped her hands on her apron and sat at one of the kitchen stools beside Autumn. "Now, tell us, dear. What happened?"

"You remember Anabeth Greenwood, the journalist who helped with Dillon Ross several months back?" Autumn poured herself a tall glass of lemonade from a pitcher and glasses left out on the island. "Turns out her cousin, Rowan, died in that fire at the university laboratory."

Penny gasped and stopped stringing up flower bundles. "Oh, dear! That's awful! My friend at the university just chatted with me about the fire. It mostly affected the chemistry department, and it burned down much of the building."

Simone tilted her head and gave them all a disbelieving face. "Well, Anabeth thought it was no accident." She grabbed an armful of plates from an upper cupboard and brought them down to the island. "And from what she told us, it did sound pretty suspicious."

"So it was arson, then?" Jo tossed a heaping salad in a large bowl as she looked up for answers.

"Well, at this point, it's really unclear whether it was arson or whether someone targeted Rowan. But, like Simone said, I'm inclined to think Anabeth is right." Autumn went for the roasted corn on the cob skewers sitting on the counter and distributed them evenly amongst all the plates. "According to Anabeth and Finn, her apprentice reporter who's also an air witch, Rowan found some very mysterious alchemical symbols around the lab, and she knew someone there had been practicing magic."

"Finn? That rings a bell." Penny swiped at the air. "Rowan was a natural-born, though, like Anabeth?" she questioned as she gathered her plate up. "Come, let's talk and eat out in the garden this evening. It's a lovely night for some firefly magic."

Autumn followed her mother out to a beautifully lit garden. The Edison light strands swung from tree to tree, and the long patio table stood dressed with small but overflowing bouquets of white wildflowers interspersed with lit white pillar candles. Lovely twine-wrapped linen napkins lay beside each place, and the scent of clover flowers danced in the air for an extra bit of happiness. She couldn't help but smile to herself and the comforting feel of this garden.

Sitting across from her mother at the table, Autumn continued. "To answer your question, yes, Rowan was a natural-born . . . As far as I know, anyway. But she got suspicious of things she saw around the lab, like the symbols. Anabeth's going to show us around her cousin's apartment, and we'll see what comes up then."

Jo and Simone pushed through the back door as Tavish trotted through their feet. The cat ran straight to the grass in the center of the garden and plopped down to be their guardian while they ate.

"Simone and I got the entire conversation from inside. No need to recount it." Jo sat at the head of the table and smoothed her skirt with her hands. "Anything else we should discuss before we get to our solstice plans?" She looked at Autumn and Simone curiously.

"Just the newest dream from James, if you wanna hear about that, too." Autumn stabbed at the asparagus tart on her plate and crammed it into her mouth as she glanced up.

"There's already been an arson and a potential murder along with it, and now James has had another one of his dreams?" Penny gulped down some lemonade. "Well, aren't we in for a full summer?"

Autumn nodded as she snapped her fingers over a pillar candle that a breeze had just blown out. Immediately, the candle relit under her fingertips. "I mean, I don't really know if the two have anything to do with each other, but yeah. He had a strange dream this time. One where he knew it was surreal but possibly still a premonition."

"That is interesting," Penny acknowledged. "When I walk within my dreams, it always feels real to me. Yet, that's probably because I'm tapping into faraway frequencies of other lands. It rarely feels like a dream when I'm immersed in it."

Jo wiped her mouth on her napkin and watched the flame Autumn had lit sway back and forth in the air once again. "Yes, in all the years I've discussed dreamwork with James's mother, Sorcha, I've never heard her speak of it being surreal. For a water witch, dreams come across just as the waking world."

"What happened in the dream, anyway?" Simone sank her teeth into a half-eaten piece of corn on the cob and propped one knee up onto her chair as she waited for an answer.

Having devoured her asparagus tart already, Autumn put her fork down to recall James's description as the flame in front of her flickered uncontrollably and lifted a thin column of smoke into the air. "A woman in the woods, moving throughout the trees, and a cauldron bubbling away in front of him as he watched."

Waving her hand in the air dismissively, Jo shook her head. "Well, that could be any of us." She stood to clear a few of the plates away as they finished. "Did he say anything more about the woman?"

"She was an older woman in dark robes, and . . . she shapeshifted in front of him." Autumn looked up at Aunt Jo, who stopped just before heading through the back door.

Jo peered over her shoulder at Penny. "A shapeshifter. That's not something I've seen in all my years, but it serves as the making of stories." She pulled the back door handle open to bring the dishes into the kitchen as she locked eyes with her sister. "Penny?"

Penny sighed and stood from the table. "Come, let's set the fireflies alight while we talk." She moved to the side of the garden where a row of tall grasses led to the bottom of the large maple tree. Crouching down, she lifted a finger toward a firefly resting on a blade of grass. She cupped it in her palm and reached it up toward Autumn behind her.

As she bent over her mother's hand, Autumn whispered under her breath. "Show us your inner glow. Light up the night and tell your friends to burn bright. Mix through the garden and in our sight take flight."

The firefly in Penny's palm made a twirling motion into the air as golden sparks followed behind it. Gradually, it lit itself and dotted the evening sky with sparks before finding several friends to do the same.

Smiling at the dozens of flickering lights highlighting the well-appointed garden, Penny stood and put a hand on Autumn's cheek. "Thank you, ladybug. I've always enjoyed watching you speak to the tiny winged energies." She brushed her palms together to dust off that task before continuing. "Now then, about this shapeshifting crone."

Simone chuckled from the table. "Aunt Penny, I love it when you're so matter of fact."

"And I, you, dear." Penny walked the center of the garden, holding her hand out for a firefly to land here and there. "We as Celtic witches have heard stories of shapeshifters passed down through time. Gods and goddesses moving through worlds, blending into their surroundings or bending situations to their will."

Setting her feet firmly on the ground and sitting up straight, Simone opened her eyes wide. "Oh, this is getting good. You have my attention."

Jo pushed through the back door and put her hands on her hips. "We'll clean the rest later. What have I missed?"

"Shape merely conforms to our world, but to a goddess . . ." Penny planted herself in one place and slid her right foot across the grass in a semicircle. A line of clover flowers bloomed on the line she had drawn. "Infinite possibilities exist. And the distinction between maiden and fox or raven and crone blur into the interchangeable."

"How would we know for sure that we're dealing with a goddess and not just a witch testing his or her powers?" Autumn bent down as Tavish pawed at her leg to be lifted. His green eyes shimmered as he looked up at her before rubbing his head across her chin with admiration.

"Goddesses do not just appear to anyone." Jo moved forward, twisting the rings on her fingers as she spoke. "A witch, however, would be evident in any form, even to the most layperson of us all." She gathered the hem of her skirt in her hand and swished it through the air as she turned toward the table. "Now, that's enough about fires and suspicious dreams for one evening. We have a solstice to plan, and I for one need to approach this fire season with calm rather than anxious energy. Let's have more gatherings with family and friends and less scurrying around town, trying to do away with dark energies, shall we?"

"Agreed," Autumn replied as she took a long sip of her lemonade. "More gathering, less scurrying . . . if we can help it. But at this rate . . ."

"Now, now." Penny walked back to the table and sat beside Jo. "Focusing on the positive to help soothe the negative."

"Well, I for one am up for a celebration, even if it is of the fire variety." Simone smiled. "As long as we can bring a bit of water into the mix as well."

"Yes, of course, dear." Jo patted her daughter's hand. "I wouldn't have it any other way. Penny and I will decorate the garden as usual, but the cauldrons will be our main focus throughout the evening. Autumn, you and Lainy can attend to those. Simone, you'll help me lead the way down to the river at dusk, and we'll dip into the water and draw down the moon to welcome in the coming darker days."

"Sounds good. I'm in for a little dip in the river and a chat with the triple goddess." Simone's eyebrows lifted as she said the words, but the idea gave Autumn an unsettled feeling.

Perking up, Autumn nodded. "I'll make sure the rest of the coven knows to attend." She couldn't help but focus on Simone's last words. "Just one thing, though. If we're gonna invoke the triple goddess, let's ask that she not take the form of a crone shapeshifting through the woods."

Chapter 4

Simone slammed the door to her black Jeep SUV and gaped at the well-maintained cedar-shingled apartment building in front of her. Putting her hands on her hips, she looked the large Craftsman-style pillars up and down around the front walkways.

"Are you sure this is the place? It's a little . . . upscale for a college student." Simone looked curiously over at Autumn.

"I'm pretty sure Rowan had some money behind her. You know Anabeth's parents are fairly well-off." Autumn walked up to the tall outdoor stairway that extended up the outer corner of the building.

Suddenly, Anabeth popped her head over the top railing on the third floor and called to them, waving. "Hey, I'm up here. Come on up."

Simone shrugged and followed Autumn up the stairs, past doorways with bronze address numbers, lantern lights next to the apartment doors, and even sculpted wooden posts at the top of each landing.

"Man, who knew college kids lived this well?" Simone jogged up the last flight of stairs and found Anabeth at the top. "Anabeth, there's no way your cousin made this kind of money from a university lab job. Was your family funding her to live here?"

Anabeth made a slight snort under her breath as she grabbed the key out of her pocket. "Yeah, she didn't mind using the family funds while she was in school, but Rowan was like me. She knew she wanted to make her own way in the world after she graduated. We talked about it a lot, actually. All the things we would do together once she finally had more freedom to live on her own terms." Anabeth pushed the front door of the apartment open and held her arm out for Autumn and Simone to come inside.

Autumn flipped on a light inside the door and found a well-appointed sitting room with large, cushioned chairs and a substantial-sized sofa in a sitting room of mostly neutral colors. "Did people know she had money?"

Nodding, Anabeth went to the kitchen to turn on the pendant lights over the island. "Yeah, they knew, but her ex Keith caused the biggest problem with it. From what Rowan told me, he was into some things that required quite a bit of up-front cash . . . to the tune of thousands of dollars that he didn't have."

"Sounds like we hit on something there. What was he into?" Simone wandered through the apartment and stopped as she came to an office space with tall bookcases and a large desk with notebooks strewn around it.

"A grow operation, apparently." Anabeth crossed her arms as she spoke. "Keith and his buddies developed some land where they grew marijuana. I guess they did pretty well except for the amount they still owed some suppliers. Rowan lived with the guy for a while, and he repeatedly tried to get money out of her. She even caught him jotting down her bank account numbers. But one day, Keith's supplier came by demanding money when Keith wasn't there. They knocked Rowan around a bit and scared her, so she reached her breaking point. Finally, she broke up with him."

"Sounds like she put up with a lot from him until she finally saw the writing on the wall." Autumn glanced through a bunch of picture frames sitting on a shelf. As she came to an overturned one, she carefully lifted it and saw a girl with a guy's arm around her at what appeared to be a campfire. Autumn turned the photo for Anabeth to see. "Is this Rowan and Keith?"

Moving closer, Anabeth squinted at the photo. "Yeah, that's them. She fell for him pretty hard at first, but over time it wore off." Anabeth tapped on the frame. "This must have been at one of the bonfires his mountain bike gang holds. They're the ones with the grow operation, and when they're not growing, they're riding."

"Mountain bikes . . . interesting." Autumn took the photo from Anabeth and placed it back on the shelf just as she had found it. "They must ride on the local mountain trails. But what about these bonfires? Where do they have those?"

Anabeth shrugged. "Honestly, who ever knows? They've got their secret spots where they like to set up. Rowan seemed kind of into the secrecy of it all, but I always told her the excitement would become more trouble than it was worth."

"Hey, come over here. I think you both should see this," Simone called from behind the large desk as she flipped through a sketchbook in her hands. She flattened the pages and held it up for them to see. "These notebooks are full of sketches. Sigils of some sort as far as I can tell."

"Sigils?" Anabeth ran her hand over a page with a dark charcoal drawing of a circle with a spiral pattern like a seashell inside of it. "I've never seen these before. What are they?"

Autumn took another notebook off the desk in front of them and flipped through several more pages of charcoal and pencil drawings. As she held the pages, the insight came to her. Rowan lived in a state of fear and confusion. "She wanted protection symbols, but someone gave her these instead."

"Autumn's right. I feel the fear seeping from the pages, and it's like the lines contain fear and confusion within them."

Simone traced a line on the page and lifted her finger to reveal a bit of charcoal on it. "These drawings aren't for protection if that's what she thought. They have a sturdy force to them, though, that's for sure. Where would she get sigils like this?"

Anabeth's eyes widened at the thought. "I have no idea." Tears formed as she looked at the drawings before her. "Why wouldn't she come to me? We told each other everything . . . Or so I thought."

Moving her arm around Anabeth's shoulder, Autumn gave her a gentle squeeze. "Sometimes people get so wrapped up in their inner worlds that they don't realize others stand right outside of it, waiting to help. I should know. I'm always in my head about things, and it takes practice to stay grounded and know that I don't have to do things all on my own." She stared down at the drawings and thought about her own magic for a moment. "That's why I'm looking to others above all now."

Simone squinted at Autumn, trying to feel out her words. First, she had asked James for space so that she could connect with her father. Now, she wanted to seek help from others above all. Granted, Autumn's transition to being the four-points witch came with significant changes. Still, Simone felt something off with her cousin that she couldn't put her finger on yet.

A sudden ringing distracted them all, and Anabeth focused on her messenger bag at the door. She walked over to retrieve a cell phone inside. "It's Rowan's phone. The coroner sent it home with me the other night when I picked up her things."

"Go ahead. Answer it." Autumn nodded for her to proceed.

Anabeth put the phone on speaker when answering. "Hello?"

"Yes, this is Dr. Ross's office calling for Rowan Stewart. Is she available, please?"

"Uh, actually, you can leave a message with me." Anabeth appeared confused as she waited.

"Please let Ms. Stewart know she has her regular appointment with us at ten tomorrow. She can call us back to confirm."

"All right, and you said this was Dr. Ross's office, correct?"

"That's right. Dr. Dillon Ross. We'll see her tomorrow."

"Okay, thank you." Anabeth ended the call and looked up at the girls in confusion.

Autumn gave Simone a knowing look and then came back to Anabeth. "Dillon Ross is James's uncle. He's a therapist here in Hollow's Glenn. She must have been seeing him to work through some of the fear."

Anabeth threw her hands up and started pacing the room. "Great, so Rowan had weird sigils all over the place and saw a therapist about something she was afraid of. What else didn't I know about?" Anabeth covered her eyes with her hands. "I could have helped her."

"She clearly had some stressful things going on that she needed to sort through. It's possible that she didn't wanna drag you into it, too." Simone tried to be reassuring, but it seemed to make Anabeth feel even worse.

"Let's just focus on what we know now and try not to play the what-if game in our minds." Autumn rubbed a hand over Anabeth's back to comfort her. "Rowan received these sigils from someone, but we don't know who. That person must have known that she was afraid of something and either amplified or potentially created the fear with these symbols. We can start with Dillon and see where that gets us. Also, we know Keith needed money and knew Rowan had lots of it. Plus, that mountain bike gang of his liked to host bonfires, so we may find something there if we can track down their whereabouts. Did Keith also have access to the university lab?"

"Yeah, I guess I didn't mention that. He's a grad student in biochemistry, so he worked in the next lab over from Rowan."

"Really?" Simone rolled her eyes. "Biochemist ex-boyfriend who needs money for his grow operation, knows Rowan has money, rides in a mountain bike gang that likes fire, and is in the lab right next to the one that conveniently got burned down? Yeah, he's suspect number one."

"It seems highly likely, but . . ." Autumn lifted the picture of Rowan and Keith from the shelf again. "What would be the motive for burning down the lab? If he wanted money, why not kill her at home where he easily had access?"

"Better coverup?" Simone suggested. "It might be easier to make the lab fire look like an accidental fire that had nothing to do with Rowan."

"She kept logs of her scholarship funds and grant money at the lab. Special accounts funded all of her research, and

Keith probably knew that." Anabeth went to the office area and pulled open a small music box from the bookshelf. She removed a key and proceeded toward a large file drawer on the left side of the desk. Opening it, she sorted through a few file folders and pulled out a document. "Here's a grant from the Casey Endowment Fund. This one alone was worth thousands of dollars."

Autumn skimmed the page and realized Rowan's research brought in significant funds to the chemistry department. "So if someone knew the extent of her grant money and how to get access to it through the accounts, they could steal the money and cover up their traces through a fire."

"Yeah, but bank accounts would be on multiple computer systems and backed up at other locations as well. How could you cover that up?" Simone questioned that theory as the girls put the apartment back together and headed for the door.

"Hackers can cover their tracks on the system so no one would know who accessed the funds and where they went." Anabeth shrugged as the girls gave her the eye. "What? I've covered a few fraud stories and learned a thing or two over the years."

Simone laughed as she closed the door behind them and trotted down the stairs. "All right, well, I guess we know who to call if we need to do some computer hacking."

"Yeah, yeah, hilarious. Anyway, what's our next move? Dr. Ross?" Anabeth's sadness seemed to dissipate, and now she was ready to get to the bottom of her cousin's case.

Autumn nodded. "Dr. Ross sounds like a good bet. I'll go over and talk with him later. Hopefully he'll be receptive to talking with me since we've gotten closer over the last several months." She paused for a moment at the bottom of the stairs and felt a warming sensation on her chest.

Her grandmother's locket pulsed under her shirt, holding her attention. Autumn tuned into the energy around her and felt the urge to face the row of large wooden pillars lining the walkway. On the nearest one, she found a bold poster stapled to it.

Simone followed her cousin's gaze curiously. "What is it?"

Autumn pointed at the poster and raised an eyebrow at the two of them. "Mountain region bike championship. Looks like it's coming up in about a week."

Crossing her arms, Simone nodded and smiled. "A bike race sounds like the perfect opportunity for a bike gang to surface."

As Autumn and Simone looked over the poster, Anabeth squinted and walked over to her car where a white paper sat face down under her windshield wiper. She tugged on the paper and read it to herself. "Dig too deeply and you'll be in over your head." Looking up as the girls came into the parking lot with her, she held up the message.

"Woah, where did you get this?" Simone grabbed the paper.

"I found it lying under my windshield wiper." Anabeth pulled out her phone and took a picture of the paper. "Someone knows we're looking into Rowan's death. And usually when someone tells me to stop digging, that means I'm on the right track."

Chapter 5

Autumn turned the dial on the radio in Simone's SUV and found a folk station that she hoped might shift the uneasy mood. She rolled down the window and let the warm breeze blow through her hair as she thought about their next move.

"Now's probably a good time for you to drop me off at Dillon's office. He'll be a friendly face to help sort things out." Autumn turned to look at her cousin in the driver's seat. "Plus, he's probably wrapping up his clients for the day, and I may be able to slide in and talk to him before he leaves."

"You want me to drop you off? You think it'll make him more receptive to talking if it's just you?" Simone made a cringing face and turned her gaze to the radio for a moment. "What is this music? I'm switching it."

Laughing at Simone's abruptness, Autumn nodded. "Yeah, I don't expect him to tell me much of anything about Rowan's therapy sessions, but I bet he'll give me something."

"Okay, he's just across from the downtown river walk, right? Maybe you can get a ride back with James. He should be finishing his work, too." Simone raised an eyebrow. "I know he'll take every opportunity he can get with you."

Autumn blushed at the thought. It made her happy to know that he felt the same way about her as she did about him. Yet, she needed this season to learn more about her father, her fae side, and to reconnect with the ancestors. She didn't want to throw all of her time with James out the window, though, but with more responsibility came tougher decisions.

She sighed and looked out the window again. "I told him I needed to take a bit of time to sort through things this summer."

Simone turned the corner, approaching the downtown square as she gave her cousin the eye. "Sort through things? Like what? He likes you a lot, and you like him, too. What do you need time for?"

"Wow, that's interesting coming from someone who always acts uninterested in the guy who's completely smitten with her. Don't pretend you're not completely into Ben, too, and don't give me this 'what do I need time for' business. You know I need to get to know my father better, not to mention figuring out how to be part fae and the four-points witch. And where are the ancestors in all of this?" Autumn threw her hands up, overwhelmed. "I don't know when I'm going to have time to solve this latest death along with running our paper shop, let alone see James."

Putting the car in park, Simone widened her eyes. "Wow, you just released one big stress ball on me." She sighed and raised a hand to motion at the side window. "Well, we're here at Dillon's. No time like the present to dive fully into a murder investigation." She turned and put her arm up on the back of her seat. "Seriously, Autumn, get out of your head and just breathe. We've been over this. You need to let your heart guide you more. And when you let your head and your heart work together, you do some pretty incredible things. So stop stressing so much and let James give you a ride home, okay? You need him to help ground you right now."

Autumn glanced across the street at the downtown revitalization project. Allan Construction had already replaced pieces of the river walk with new stamped concrete. She could see James overseeing the work down by the water. As she looked at him, something immediately told her they had plenty of time together. Their story had only just begun.

"You're right." Autumn shook her head and looked back at her cousin as she grabbed her backpack. "I do need to tap into my heart more, but not today. James and I have lots of time together ahead, and right now I need to focus." Autumn slid out of the SUV and gave Simone a wave. "Thanks, cuz. I'll see you in a bit, hopefully with more information."

"You better." Simone rolled down the driver's side window and peeked out. "Oh, and I'm making veggie lasagna tonight, so hurry. I've been craving it for days, and I'm not above eating without you."

"Got it," Autumn replied with a laugh as she headed up the steps into Dillon Ross's office building.

The red stone building sat on the historic street of the downtown square. Green vines covered the red exterior, while on the inside, a more formal white marble tile lined the hallway. She admired the charm of the building and wondered how she'd never been inside before. As she perused a wall directory for Dillon's name, someone passed behind her, nudging her forward.

"Oh, excuse me, dear," a familiar voice said behind Autumn before putting a hand on her shoulder. "Autumn! Hello again."

"Dr. Carmichael, hi. What are you doing over here?" Autumn gave her a curious look.

"I know. I'm always glued to the hospital." Rose Carmichael waved a hand in the air. "I just needed to speak with Dillon Ross about a few things and thought I'd get some fresh air. It's such a lovely day, and I'm excited for summer. But enough about me, how's your mother? I haven't seen her since the party she hosted for her new tea collection."

Autumn nodded with pride at how her mother blossomed after coming back home from years away. "She's doing great. The teas have been selling like hotcakes in the shop, and she has several clients for her holistic medicine services. I think she's settling back into town nicely."

"Oh, that's wonderful to hear, dear. Give her my best, will you?" Dr. Carmichael began walking away, when Autumn reached out to stop her.

"Actually, I hoped to see you soon." Autumn stepped in closer. "There's something I need to ask you, and your nephew, Finn, thought you could give me some insight."

Rose lifted an eyebrow and looked at Autumn with concern. "Finn? I see. If it's anything like the last time the founders got together, then . . ."

Putting her hand on Dr. Carmichael's arm, Autumn shook her head. "No, it's not that dire . . . At least I don't think so at this point. But it is a sensitive matter that we should talk about in private."

"All right, why don't you have your mother message me? I think I have some time tomorrow for lunch. I could stop by the house if that's best." Dr. Carmichael gave Autumn a tight-lipped smile and began walking out. "Just let me know. It was good seeing you, Autumn."

With a sigh, Autumn regrouped and focused on Dillon Ross's office. She made her way up one flight of painted white wooden stairs and found a sign on a half-glass, half-wooden door that read Dr. Dillon Ross, Psychologist.

As she made her way inside, the receptionist immediately looked up from what she was doing to greet her. "Hi, how may I help you?"

"Hi, I'm Autumn MacKinnon, and I was hoping . . ."

"Autumn?" Dillon's voice trailed in from around the corner. He walked through a frosted glass door beside the reception desk and opened his arms wide to give her a hug. "It is you! Stacy, this is Autumn, the one who helped save my life, and now she's dating my nephew. She never has to wait in this office." He tapped the corner of his nose with his pointer finger and winked at the receptionist.

Stacy smiled and nodded. "Of course, Dr. Ross. Autumn, you're welcome here anytime."

"Now, come on back." Dillon waved at Autumn to follow him through the frosted glass door and into his office at the back. "I'm just getting my things together for the evening. Abigail expects me soon, as we're having James's parents over for dinner. Please sit and tell me what brings you by." He motioned to a chair in front of a large wooden desk and a wall of single-hung wooden windows.

As Autumn sat, Dillon propped himself up on the edge of his desk and crossed his arms, waiting for her to begin. "Right, well, as usual, I'm afraid I'm here with a bit of bad news. One of your patients, Rowan Stewart, died in a fire at the university a few days back."

"Oh my! I saw an article about it in *The Glenn Herald*, but I didn't put two and two together that she might have been there." Dillon shook his head as he stared at the floor in thought. "How did you know she was a patient of mine?"

"I was with her cousin, Anabeth, when a call came in from your office on Rowan's cell phone, which Anabeth now has in her possession. Apparently Rowan had an appointment scheduled with you." Autumn watched Dillon's reaction, gauging how willing he may be to open up about her.

Dillon stood up and paced a bit before looking out the window to the street below. "Yeah, she had been seeing me for several months now." He turned and gave Autumn a serious look. "The fire at the university, what caused it?"

Autumn tilted her head and paused for a moment in consideration of how to put it. "Originally the police thought it was an accident, but it's looking more like arson now. Plus . . ."

"You think someone targeted Rowan in the fire." Dillon chewed on his bottom lip as he considered the implications of the idea.

"Yes, that's right. Anabeth asked me to look into it since some suspicious activity surrounded Rowan at the time of her death." Autumn sat up straighter in her chair, preparing to give the details of the case. "For example, Rowan took some photos of strange alchemical symbols at the lab before she died, and we found lots of sigil-style drawings in her apartment. I'm trying to make sense of what happened and find anyone who may have wanted to harm her."

"Well, Autumn, you know I trust you implicitly, but I cannot reveal the details of my sessions with Rowan. However . . ." Dillon sat at his desk and started opening something on his computer. He turned the screen to show Autumn a university news article about a previous lab fire. "This latest fire wasn't the only occurrence."

Squinting at the screen, Autumn scooted to the edge of her chair. "There was a previous fire." She read the headline aloud. "Chemistry lab fire burns one and causes disruptions."

"Check with Chief Walsh. See if he might give you access to some of Rowan's correspondence, including any complaints around this smaller fire. From what I remember, it was a close call, and she sustained some large burns." He sat back in his wooden swivel chair and rocked. "Now, about those drawings . . . If I were you, I'd look for someone close to her who knew symbology. Someone willing to offer assistance to get in her good graces."

Nodding along, Autumn followed his train of thought. "Someone with what appeared to be a protection sigil for whatever she was afraid of at the lab."

Dillon shrugged and stood up to come around the desk. "That's where I would start."

Autumn gave him a hug before heading to the office door. "Thanks, Dillon. I appreciate your help."

He lifted a finger and stopped for a moment. "Oh, and just so you know. It's likely there's a witch or two working in that lab. In all honesty, I think Rowan caught on to it, and maybe that's where some of this came from, but just . . . be careful and don't assume anything. We wouldn't want anything to happen to our four-points witch."

"I'll be careful." Autumn smiled at him as he opened the office door. "Give my best to Abigail and James's parents."

She headed out of the office, stopping to say goodbye at the reception counter before moving out into the stairway. As she peered out the stairway window to the fountain square across the street, her eye went to her grandmother's bench by the river.

"I need some help with this one, Gran," Autumn whispered to herself, when in response the scent of iris flowers filled the stairway around her. She smiled with comfort, knowing that Gran was, in fact, there. "Your iris flowers always give me hope and a little insight. Thanks for that."

Sighing, she moved her gaze to the construction site with James beside it. "I guess Simone is right. My head and my heart need to work together more." The iris scent grew stronger with her words, and she pulled out her phone to call James.

"Hey, it's me. You know how I said I needed space for a while?" She smiled as she trotted down the stairs and listened to his voice on the other end of the phone. "Yeah, you shouldn't always listen to me. Look across the street."

She pulled the office building door open and walked out onto the curb, waving to him at the bottom of the hill across the street. The iris scent grew stronger in the air, and Autumn felt the wind pick up around her. The call of the ancestors began whispering softly on the wind and getting louder, only to be heard by her. Autumn closed her eyes and tuned into them for the first time in a long time.

"Mend the heart. Dissolve the menacing mind."

Autumn stood rooted to the curb. While grateful to actually hear their familiar voices once again, she knew they brought warnings.

James approached and eyed her curiously. "Everything okay? What's going on?" He gave her a slight smile, unsure of what to make of her standing there.

Nodding, she reached up to kiss him. "Yeah, everything's great." Looking into his eyes, she felt how much he meant to her. It wasn't her own heart the ancestors had warned about mending. Someone else's heart had broken, and if she didn't find out who, the lab fire might only be the beginning.

Chapter 6

Autumn woke to the sound of rain tapping against her window in the middle of the night. Her eyes opened sleepily as she watched it drip down the center of the glass pane in between her curtains. Tavish sauntered up to her face and pressed his wet nose against her cheek.

"I know, Tav. You're up for your midnight snack and want some company." She rubbed the edge of his ear as he continued to nudge her cheek.

Pausing for a moment, she gained a bit more consciousness. "Or are you and the rain trying to tell me something?"

The cat jumped down off the bed, and Autumn felt compelled to follow him to the window. She slowly dragged the curtains to the side and peered out into the dark, rainy night. As she pressed her fingertips to the glass and watched the raindrops, she received a download.

"Anabeth." Autumn looked down at Tavish sitting beside her. The cat lifted its front paws to rest on the windowsill in front of him, and they both stared out into the dark.

Autumn pressed her whole hand more firmly to the windowpane and felt a pulse of energy course through her. She immediately saw a vision of the black tourmaline pendulum that Anabeth had taken home from the shop.

"I think something's wrong, Tav. Anabeth needs help." Autumn hurried out of her bedroom to go wake Simone.

As soon as she opened the door to the hallway, she found Simone pulling on a pair of black leggings under her long black tunic T-shirt.

"Something's up," Simone said as she tied a knot into the lower corner of her T-shirt to tailor it a bit. "A very adamant spirit interrupted my sleep, and I'm fairly sure it was Rowan."

"Rowan?" Autumn followed her cousin's lead and grabbed a pair of leggings and a more presentable T-shirt from her dresser drawer. "She's here now?"

"Yep. I think she hovered near my nightstand until I finally woke up. She's giving me the sense of Anabeth's aura, and something about it seems urgent."

Autumn tied her long auburn hair back into a loose bun and headed toward the door. "I felt it, too. The rain on the window woke me up, and I had a vision of that pendulum I gave her. Something's not right."

"Wait, you had a vision? Not just knowing something?" Simone grabbed her black rain boots and threw them on before grabbing the car keys.

"I've had more visions lately. I'll tell you on the way. Let's just get to Anabeth." Autumn gave Tavish a quick chin scratch as they opened the front door. "Thanks for nudging me to the window, Tav. Enjoy your midnight snack, and I'll be back soon."

Simone grabbed a long umbrella from a wall hook beside the door, and they both headed out underneath it into the night.

"Sure would be nice if the rain could die down a bit for us." Autumn raised her eyebrows at her cousin, who fumbled around with the car keys as her phone buzzed in her pocket.

Sighing, Simone unlocked the SUV for Autumn to jump inside. "Give me a minute, geez. I just woke up to Rowan's spirit energy forcing me out the door."

Pulling her phone out of her pocket as she hurried around to the driver's side door, Simone noticed a text from Finn. She slid into the driver's seat and shook off the umbrella, throwing it behind her and slamming the door. "It's Finn. How did he get my number?"

Autumn looked at her cousin with concern. "Anabeth told him to call."

Simone scanned the message quickly. "Something's happened at Anabeth's house, and she's asking for us."

"A middle of the night text saying Anabeth needs us? That's not like her at all." Autumn's face grew solemn.

"We better get over there," Simone said hurriedly as she pulled the car away from Hawthorn Cottage and down the tree-lined road toward town. "Let me just center my energy, and I'll take care of this rain." She peered over the steering wheel up to the sky outside. "Man, I didn't realize it was supposed to rain tonight. The sky knows something we don't."

Simone took a deep breath and let it out as she smoothed her right hand across the air in front of her. "Close the skies. Calm the rain. Help is on the way. Let us now ease the fray." She continued to move her hand across the air in a straight line, as if smoothing a blanket, and the raindrops slowly dissipated in front of them. "There. That's better."

"You think the rain activated to get our attention and warn us of whatever's happening with Anabeth?" Autumn searched her backpack for some peppermints their coven sister Eve had made for the intention of clarity. She opened a small silver tin and lifted it up for Simone to take one as well.

"Probably." Simone nodded. "Between the rain and Rowan sitting in my bedroom, the elements and the ancestors know how to get our attention now." She pulled the SUV around the corner onto Anabeth's street and pointed her finger toward Anabeth's house.

"The police are here." Autumn sat up in her seat and pressed her forearms onto the dashboard. "Just park on the street and we'll walk up."

"Okay, sounds good." Simone ran the windshield wipers one last time as she parked the car on the curb. "I see Ben out there. He rarely works nights anymore unless it's something important."

"And there's Finn sitting with Anabeth on the front step. I'll head over to them while you talk with Ben." Autumn pushed her way out of the car and walked between a few police officers before waving to Finn.

"What's going on? Anabeth, are you all right?" Autumn crouched down on the ground in front of them.

Shaking her head, Anabeth opened up her palm to reveal the black tourmaline pendulum shimmering with golden sparks of magic. "I'm not sure. I'm still shaking."

"Someone tried to break into her house while she was asleep, but they were unsuccessful." Finn pursed his lips as he gave Autumn a serious look. "I heard the call come in on my police scanner, so I came over right away. She wanted me to call you and Simone, too."

Anabeth ran her fingers over the crystal and pulled it up to her chest. "If I hadn't put up this pendulum you gave me, then I don't know what would've happened." She turned around and pointed to the door behind her.

Autumn sighed with relief. "The black tourmaline protected you." She smiled as she watched the hints of shimmering magic dot around the crystal. "When Simone charged it under the last full moon, I knew this crystal needed to keep someone safe. I'm just glad I gave it to you in the shop the other day. The tourmaline found its way to you when you needed it most."

"Well, I'm glad I took it. Whoever tried to break in went to the front door first, which is where I hung the pendulum. I heard them struggling, but when they couldn't get in, there were strange sweeping sounds around the doorway. Then, they came around to the side window, and I heard the noises again."

Behind her a couple officers were scraping paint chips from Anabeth's front door into an evidence bag. "You're lucky they didn't get in, ma'am," one of them interjected.

Simone squinted and took a step up to the porch. "What's that you're scraping into the bag?"

The officer shrugged at her. "Don't know, exactly, but it sure smells like salt. We'll send it to the lab to confirm. It's best you move aside while we clear the scene, and then she can go back inside for the night."

Autumn opened her arms to guide the others to sit in the dark on the grass. As they sat, Autumn stared at the front door and received a download. "That's what you heard them doing when they couldn't get in . . . creating a marking of some kind."

"Marking?" Anabeth's chest grew tight. "You mean, like the symbols we found all over Rowan's apartment?"

"Maybe . . . I felt a darker undertone there as well, but the drawings at Rowan's carried an energy that suggested confusion to me." Simone wrapped her arms around her knees and stared at the house as well.

"Yeah, we thought they were sigils, but I don't think they are. It's coming through as some kind of marking, though. And the salt smell . . ." Autumn trailed off while looking at Finn.

Sighing, Finn ran his fingers through his dark-blond hair before explaining. "Salt serves as one of the three main primes of alchemy. As far as I know, it represents the body in physical form." They all stared at him with curiosity, and he cleared his throat. "What? I told you I learned some stuff from my aunt. Plus"—he shrugged and looked at Autumn—"I have a pretty strong photographic memory. I mean, better than photographic, really. So, I pick stuff up."

Simone raised her eyebrows. "Okay, note to self. Remember to hide all personal information when you're around."

Finn lifted his palms in innocence. "Look, I'm just trying to help, okay?" Pointing to the pendulum in Anabeth's hands, he added, "I think you better add a little something extra to that thing, and Anabeth shouldn't stay here by herself."

"You're right," Autumn agreed. "Anabeth, where can you stay for a few days?"

"Um, I guess I could stay with my mom for a while. Finn can drive me over there." Anabeth raised the pendulum in the air. "And I'll bring this along with me."

"Before you do, we'll enhance the protection spell like Finn suggested." Autumn sat down in the grass beside Simone. She took the pendulum from Anabeth and laid it over the blades of grass between Simone and her. Grabbing her cousin's hands, she nodded and whispered under her breath so no one else on the property could hear. "Earth below, strengthen this pendulum with your protection. Keep the bearer safe from harm until it returns to me as the giver. By my words and the power of us two, make it so."

Glancing down, Autumn watched as golden sparks danced around the pendulum and sparked off into the grass. She smiled at her magic and picked it up to give back to Anabeth. "Just as you did before, keep it where you'd like to create a boundary. It'll protect you until you're ready to send it back to me."

Anabeth gave Autumn a serious look and took the pendulum. "It's already protected me once, so I know what it can do. Thank you."

"Autumn." Finn tilted his head for Autumn to join him a few steps away, and she followed. The police cleared the way in front of Anabeth's door, and Finn motioned for Autumn to look at it once again. "Now what do you see at the base of Anabeth's front door?"

Autumn moved a few steps closer to the front porch and peered around a few officers. The porch light illuminated the doorway enough for her to run her eyes down the entirety of it. "I see . . . some kind of symbol painted on the bottom of the door. It's faint, but is that a circle with a line through the middle of it?"

Finn nodded in confirmation. "That's right." He ran his hands through his hair once more. "The alchemical symbol for salt. Looks like someone painted it on the door."

"So someone marked it with an alchemical symbol?" Autumn met eyes with Finn.

"Yeah, that's my guess," he said. "The fire inspector also just confirmed that the lab fire was no accident. They're looking at it as arson now. With Anabeth's house being marked with salt on top of our suspicions about the fire, we need to speak with my aunt, Rose."

Autumn nodded. "My mother invited her to tea, so I'll speak with her tomorrow. What do you think she'll say?"

Letting out a laugh under his breath, Finn shoved his hands in his jeans pockets. "She'll say what she always taught me, that alchemy unfolds over a lifetime of study, practice, and integration. Those who pursue it too quickly lack enough empathy for the power they wield. Those who wield it without first becoming it risk consequences harsher than their comprehension."

"And which do you think we're dealing with here?" Autumn searched Finn's eyes for the answer, and they both responded at once.

"Both."

Eve's Lemon Blackberry Cake For Connection Across The Veil

For the cake:

3 cups flour

2 tsp baking powder

1 tsp baking soda

½ tsp salt

1 ¼ cups sugar

½ cup yogurt or sour cream

3/4 cup unsalted butter, room temperature

3 lemons, zest only

¼ cup lemon juice

3 eggs, whole

1 egg white

1 cup buttermilk, or 1 Tbsp vinegar plus milk to make 1 cup

For the filling:

1 cup sugar

1/4 cup water

4 cups fresh blackberries (or frozen)

1 Tbsp lemon juice

For the cream cheese frosting:

1 cup unsalted butter, room temperature

8 oz cream cheese, room temperature

6 cups powdered sugar

1 lemon, zest and juice

Preheat the oven to 350 degrees Fahrenheit. Generously butter three round cake pans to reduce sticking.

In a large bowl, mix together all dry cake ingredients except the sugar. Tap the bowl on the counter three times while saying,

As below, so above. With the ingredients of the earth, we open to other worlds with love.

Set the mixture aside while you combine the other ingredients.

Gather the wet ingredients and sugar for the cake. Use a mixer to beat together the butter and yogurt until creamy in texture. Add lemon zest and juice, continuing to mix. Then, add one egg at a time and beat for a couple of minutes.

Combine half of the dry ingredients into the wet mixture. As you mix, say aloud,

I mix to open. I mix to invite.

Mix until incorporated, and then add half of the buttermilk. Continue mixing while adding the last half of the dry ingredients and the last half of the buttermilk.

Divide the batter evenly between the three round pans, filling about ¾ of the way full.

Bake for 20 minutes, or until a toothpick inserted comes out clean. Let the cakes rest in the pans for 15 minutes before transferring to a wire rack.

For the filling, heat the sugar and water in a saucepan over medium heat. After the sugar begins dissolving, add the blackberries and lemon juice. Gently mash the berries as they heat up. As you mash, say aloud,

May this filling of mine connect and reveal. Drop the veil and no longer conceal.

Envision the veil across the earthly plane dissolving and the surrounding energies becoming visible. Mash the berries until no large pieces remain.

When the mixture has thickened, after about five minutes or more, remove from the heat and let cool. Pour into a glass bowl and set aside.

In a medium bowl, beat the butter and cream cheese together with a mixer until smooth. Add in the powdered sugar and combine. Next, add the lemon juice and zest, mixing for a minute until fluffy. Do not over whip.

Once the cakes have cooled, place a couple small drops of frosting on a cake plate and lift the first cake round on to secure it. Level the top of the cake with a serrated knife if necessary. Then, use about ¼ of the frosting to spread a layer onto the top of the cake and to pipe an edge around the circle.

Spread half of the filling on top of the frosting. Pause for a moment and gaze at the deep blackberry filling and repeat this phrase three times:

With each bite, the veil will drop until the partaker would like it to stop.

Then, place the second cake round on top and repeat the process with this layer and the third. Carefully, spin the cake plate around in a clockwise direction three times, snapping your fingers beside the cake after each turn.

Cool the cake completely before frosting the top and sides of the cake with the remaining frosting. To decorate, add a few fresh blackberries, lemon slices, or lemon zest to the top of the cake. Enjoy!

Chapter 7

Simone yawned as she felt the buzzing of her phone between her leg and the driver's seat of her SUV. She tugged on the phone while peering out the front windshield onto the police scene wrapping up at Anabeth's house. "My mom's texting me at three in the morning." She pushed back firmly into her seat and let out a deep breath.

Autumn sat in the passenger seat beside her, completely exhausted. They both met eyes after making the realization. "She knows."

Sitting up straighter in the driver's seat, Simone texted her mother that they'd be over in a minute. She didn't want her up for the rest of the night worrying about them. So the quickest way to put her at ease would be to go over to Crescent House, Penny and Jo's home.

"All right, I messaged her." Simone put the car in drive and headed toward her mother's house.

In just a few minutes, the girls arrived to see Jo waiting on the front porch for them. She sat in an evergreen wicker chair under the long lantern lights of the porch. Her arms wrapped around a fuzzy cream shawl over her nightgown, and she had a worried look on her face.

"Oh, I'm so glad you're finally here." Jo stood up from her place on the porch and held the door open for them. "Come inside, and I'll pour us some tea. The cards await."

Simone turned and gave Autumn an exasperated look. "Mom, can this wait 'til tomorrow? I just wanna go back to the cottage and crawl into bed."

Jo patted her daughter's forearm and continued through the house to the kitchen. "Spirits speak to us most in the in-between hours, dear. You know that."

Autumn smiled to herself as she followed them into the kitchen. She grabbed a few tea mugs from an upper glass-door cabinet as Jo grabbed the already hot tea kettle.

Penny trailed down the creaky stairs in her green velvet bathrobe and her hair in a long, low braid. "Good heavens, what're we all doing at this hour of the night?" She stared at Jo for a moment, and Jo gave her the eye. "Oh, dear. Something's happened."

"I felt the girls drawn out into the night, and I sensed it had something to do with this latest case." Jo stirred her own tea and tapped the antique spoon against the lip of the mug before sipping.

"Anabeth's house almost got broken into." Simone grabbed a tea mug and started sipping as well.

"Almost?" Penny questioned.

"Yeah, whoever it was didn't get in." Autumn went to the pantry hutch on a small side wall and pulled out a box of chocolate shortbread cookies. "Thankfully, I gave her a black tourmaline pendulum to hang above the door, and she used it." She laid the cookies out nicely on a tea saucer and slid it to the center of the kitchen island for everyone to partake.

"Well, good thinking on your part." Penny sipped some hot tea from a spoon in her own mug. "The tourmaline did its job to block out all the negative energy."

"True, but they sure scared Anabeth, and I'm not even sure they intended to get in." Autumn munched on a cookie as she thought.

"Oh, what makes you say that?" Jo watched her niece for a moment and let her intuition speak to her. "Something about the house."

Simone huffed under her breath. "I'd say. She had some kind of weird salt markings painted all over her front door. Apparently they're alchemical."

"Oh, Mother Moon! So this does relate to the case." Jo fidgeted with a few rings on her fingers and stared down at the counter.

"Well, let's not give this harmful alchemy any more power than it's asking for." Penny put her tea mug down and pressed her palms firmly into the kitchen counter. "Josephine, I see that you have your tarot cards out. Why don't you read for us?"

"Wonderful idea, Pen." Jo reached her hand out, and Penny nudged the tarot deck over to her sister using her tea mug, careful not to taint them with her own energy.

Jo knocked on the deck with her knuckles to clear its energy and gave the cards a shuffle. "Now, then." She closed her eyes and breathed deeply for a moment. "Water within me, see below the surface. Show us what we must know for the coming days."

Opening her eyes, Jo splayed the cards out in a fan across the counter. She nodded to Autumn to choose a card. Autumn hovered her hand across the cards and then pulled one from the side closest to her. She handed it over to Jo face down.

Flipping the card over, Jo displayed it on the counter for all to see. It depicted a blindfolded woman bound with white ribbons standing among a line of swords. "Eight of swords. A trapped and restricted energy."

Simone sighed and slid onto one of the kitchen stools. "Great. I could've told us that."

Jo shushed her daughter and returned her focus to the card. She ran a ringed finger across the image. "There is powerlessness here, yes. Things appear to be hopeless and like there is no support to find a way out." She tapped a finger over the woman's face. "However, we can remove the blindfold. If we choose to take our power back instead of giving it away, then the change we seek may very well arrive."

Penny glanced over at Autumn, eyeing the card on the table. "Everything is a matter of perspective, and we hold the keys to our own destinies."

Simone chewed on a fingernail as she considered everything said. She popped up from her stool and took one last swig from her tea. "All right, that's enough divination for one exhausting night. It's time we head home."

"Just keep the card in mind, girls." Jo gave Simone and Autumn a serious look as she came around the island to hug each of them. "Don't let the will of others dictate your own power."

"Got it, Mom." Simone kissed her mother's cheek and gave her aunt a hug.

Autumn thanked Aunt Jo and hugged her mother as well. "I'll be back tomorrow for tea with Dr. Carmichael."

Penny smiled. "I look forward to it, dear. Put some lavender under your pillow and get some rest for now."

The girls walked out to the front porch, and Jo closed the front door behind them. Autumn wrapped her arms against the large pillar beside the railing. She looked out at the black starry sky above.

"There's something else bothering you. Spill." Simone nudged her cousin with her shoulder.

"It's just . . ." Autumn plopped down on the top step and slung her arms over her knees. "I haven't heard the ancestors much until earlier today. It's like they went on vacation, and they just popped in for a quick hello before leaving again."

Simone shrugged. "That doesn't sound like the ancestors. They wouldn't just ditch you, Autumn." Simone gave her a look. "But . . . when you go through major transitions, your guides usually change along with you. Didn't you say you've been seeing more visions lately? Maybe that's how they want to communicate now."

"Yeah, maybe you're right. I have been seeing more than hearing." Autumn raked a hand through her hair. "I just assumed the ancestors would always speak to me. I've heard their voices for as long as I can remember. Sure, they've been absent for a while before, but . . . this feels different. Almost like I reach out and I can't find them. Even today, when I heard them, they felt distant."

"Is that why you wanted some time to get to know your fae side more and connect with your father?" Simone raised an eyebrow and waited silently for a response.

Autumn sighed and looked up at the stars again. "Maybe, but I don't wanna lose the witch side of me, either. I feel something changing in me, though. I'm just not sure if it's a good thing or a bad thing."

Simone stood up and brushed off the back of her tunic shirt. "There's no good or bad, cuz. Only neutral, or gray, as I like to think of it." She smirked and held out a hand to help Autumn hoist herself up. As she wrapped her arm around Autumn's shoulders, they walked back to the SUV.

"You used to wanna handle everything yourself, Miss Type-A Air Witch. Now look at you, begging the ancestors for support. My, my, how the mighty have fallen." Simone chuckled, and Autumn gave her a light punch to the ribs. "Hey, take it easy."

Simone unlocked the car, and they both hopped in. "Seriously, though, our gifts change as we change."

Nodding, Autumn knew her cousin was right. Yet as she looked out the window into the black night, she couldn't help but feel the powerlessness that Jo's tarot card had shown so clearly.

Chapter 8

The tea kettle whistled on the stove in the kitchen of Crescent House, Jo and Penny's Victorian home. Jo perked up from tying long strands of herbs together and made her way to the stove. Smiling, she lifted her head, waiting for something. "Rose is at the door, dears. Would someone mind getting it?" She carefully removed the tea kettle from the stove as the doorbell chimed. "There it is."

"I'll let her in," Penny called as she walked into the entrance hall to open the door. "Rose! It's so good to see you, friend. Come in and sit."

Rose Carmichael hugged her and nodded in thanks. "Lovely to see you, Penny." She walked into the front sitting room as she had done many times before. "As much as I'd love to sit and talk for hours, I know the girls have a few important things in mind. Not to mention, I only have a clear calendar for the next hour, if that. Hopefully we can make it short and sweet this time, although I do love our long chats."

Penny sat down beside her friend on the sofa and patted Rose's knee. "Oh, I know, but you're right. We have important matters to discuss today, as it seems has been the case quite often lately."

Jo strolled in with a large tray full of teacups and plates with small scones daintily placed on them. "Here we are. Chamomile tea with orange blossom scones for good fortune and comfort. Rose, tell us. How are you, dear?"

Autumn and Simone trailed in and sat around the bottom of the large fireplace as Rose started in.

"Ah, well, things are going smoothly at the hospital, and I have my nephew in town now to keep me on my toes. He's staying with us while he decides whether to remain long-term and work for the local paper."

"Right, I remember him. Finn, is it?" Penny questioned.

"That's right, Finn, my sister's boy. He used to stay with me for the summers occasionally while his parents did archeological research abroad." Rose picked up a teacup and a scone as she continued. "He told me something's come up here in

Hollow's Glenn that may require my expertise. Something about alchemy?"

"Yes, Dr. Carmichael." Autumn sat up straighter to speak. "Finn mentioned you knew a bit about ancient alchemy. We believe it's behind the recent fire at the university lab that resulted in the death of a girl who worked there. She was the cousin of Anabeth Greenwood, the reporter who Finn works alongside."

"Oh my." Rose put down her tea and crossed her legs. "What makes you think the fire involved alchemy?"

Autumn swallowed hard before continuing. "Rowan, the girl who died in the fire, suspected magical workings at the lab. She sent an image of alchemical symbols to Anabeth before she died. We found all kinds of drawings in her apartment as well. Plus, Anabeth's house almost got broken into last night, and whoever was there marked her house with a symbol for salt."

Rose sat back against the sofa and rubbed the top of her leg as she thought. "Well, there's no telling what we're dealing with here."

Penny put a hand on Rose's shoulder. "Let's start with the alchemy itself, then. Rose, I know you've studied this at length. What can you tell us about the ancient ways?"

"I've always loved knowing where we come from. History and the ancient ways always fascinated me, as I have a scientific brain, and I like to know how things work." Rose moved to the base of the hearth with her teacup and scone in hand as she sat. She waved to invite Autumn to join her.

"Ancient alchemy aims to transmute energy." Rose lifted the teacup. "Go ahead and blow on it."

Autumn pursed her lips and blew over the top of the water as steam rose above it with tiny golden specks of magic trailing into the air.

Smiling, Rose continued. "Now, send them into the hearth to start the fire."

Focusing on the specks of glimmering steam, Autumn directed her attention to the inside of the hearth and whispered, "From water to air and air to fire, with my words, create my desire."

The specks drifted across the air in front of them and into the bottom of the fire, where they gathered on top of a large log, igniting it with a spark.

Rose glanced around the room at all of their faces. "As our four-points witch, Autumn holds within her much of the same capabilities as an ancient alchemist. She can combine or transform energy at will, although all the energy rests within her already. For an alchemist, they must learn to manipulate it outside of themselves."

Simone nodded and looked into the fire that Autumn had created from the steam off a teacup. "I've seen her turn water into air. I'd seen nothing like it before. But if she can do that as the four-points witch wielding all the elements, then how can anyone else? And why would they, if not just for the power of it?"

"Autumn transmutes the energy because it lies within your bloodline's capacity as the original elemental witches." Rose swept a hand through the air to reference all the MacKinnon women sitting before her. "The ancients dealt with the elements in similar ways that we witches do today. However, their intent focused on perfecting the energy. Whereas we aim to maintain balance and harmony in the mountain region, the ancients sought the means to extend life, cure disease, and even establish immortality. That is, of course, part of what intrigued me as a doctor."

"Great, so you're saying someone can play the gods with alchemy." Simone threw her hand up and rolled her eyes. "No big deal."

Autumn looked further into the fire. "But are we dealing with another witch getting in over his or her head with things beyond their capabilities? Or is ancient alchemy something that anyone could have access to?"

Lifting a finger, Rose turned to face the center of the group. "Therein lies the question. The collective has widely known of alchemy for centuries. So the possibility exists for a natural-born person to learn it. Yet, without a doubt, a witch who truly understood it could dramatically amplify their powers. Either way, to wield it properly . . ."

Autumn eyed the last of the tea, which she had mostly turned into sparks minutes ago, as a vision came to her mind. A cozy cave, lit only by firelight and tall pillar candles, shone in her mind. She looked deeper into the cup, and a flash of ancient books piled high with runes surrounding them came to the forefront of her mind. "It takes training and knowledge." She finished Dr. Carmichael's thought and swallowed hard before looking at her mother.

"Tell us what just came to you, dear." Penny eyed her daughter, knowing she had received some insight.

"A mysterious cave with ancient books and runes." Autumn turned to see Tavish trotting through the doorway straight for her lap. She rubbed his head and thought for a moment. "Is there a place tucked away that has the knowledge we need?"

Jo exchanged glances with Rose and nodded. "The elder of the wood. I haven't thought of him for decades now."

Rose opened her mouth to speak but paused to consider Jo's suggestion. "I hesitated to bring him up, but he mentored me in my younger days. I feel I may have disappointed him when I decided to practice Western medicine. If he's still here, then he can lead you in the right direction. However, I'd caution you that you are not yet ready for his counsel."

Jo chuckled as she took a sip of tea. "Arailt is a temperamental one. I wouldn't go to him unless you're ready for a little squabbling."

"He chose to live as a hermit in the woods all these years, and I know his wife died a while back." Rose stood and placed the teacup on the coffee table tray. "As a wise one who has seen many centuries, the elder does not take to conversation easily. Go with clarified questions and be prepared for cagey answers in return."

"So we should be clear, but this centuries-old alchemist in a cave won't be clear with us?" Simone leaned in to tear off a piece of a scone before getting up.

"If he remains in the wood, you'll find what you need to know there. But only when you have proper questions ready for answers." Rose headed toward the hallway as they all got up to walk her out. "And please, if you go, tell him Rosemary still thinks of him fondly."

Simone drove down the tree-lined path to Hawthorn Cottage, and she and Autumn both sighed at the welcoming sight of lollipop-shaped maples dancing in the evening breeze.

"Man, I'm glad we don't have to open the shop today." Simone rolled the window down a little more and breathed deeply. "Rain's coming, and it's the perfect Sunday afternoon for some painting." She turned to look at her cousin. "Maybe it'll help me de-stress from all this alchemy business."

"Yeah, tell me about it." Autumn watched the trees pass as they drove closer to the cottage, each leaf shaking with a bit of a golden shimmer to welcome them home. "I think I'll head into the woods before the rain comes. Clear my head and talk to the earth."

As they approached the cottage, the girls watched the woman they'd known as their neighbor, Mrs. Pendleton, head into the woods between their cottage and hers. Autumn glimpsed a few blue wisps following her footsteps as she moved across the earth to the trees ahead.

"On second thought"—Autumn quickly got out of the car as Simone parked, and Tavish hopped out right behind her—"this might be my chance to see him again." She dropped her backpack on the front porch and hurried to see several firefly-like lights showing up between the trees. The cat ran ahead and swiveled around, chasing a light that encircled his tail.

"Say hi to your dad for me." Simone waved into the air and then headed up the porch steps. "I guess I've got the house to myself for some painting."

Autumn followed a few more wisps further into the tree line and found Mrs. Pendleton, really her great-aunt Freya, standing beside a circle of sparkling green mushrooms at the base of the hawthorn tree. As Mrs. Pendleton turned and stepped aside, she revealed a tall man with glowing skin and long blond hair.

"Hello again . . . Laith and Aunt Freya." Autumn took a step forward, unsure of what to do next.

"Autumn." Laith bowed his head to her and looked between the two women.

Mrs. Pendleton came toward her with open arms. "Autumn, my nephew came to connect with you more. If you wish, you may call him *athaie*, which means father in the fae language. Please, come." The woman Autumn had come to understand as the aunt watching over her all those years now beckoned her forward.

Stepping face-to-face with her father, Autumn nodded. "It's good to see you again, *Athaie*. I wondered when you might show up in these woods."

Laith nodded and bent down to the ground. He moved his hand across the brilliant green mushrooms, and they rose taller under his fingers. "The woods will announce my coming. Look to the wisps that lead to the sacred tree. I will present myself here."

"I hoped we could speak more frequently about the fae and your lands. I'd like to know more of who I am." Autumn knelt beside him, and several wisps landed on her arm. Immediately their color changed from an electric blue to a sunburst yellow, and Tavish sniffed his nose at them.

"Oh." Laith chuckled at the sight. "They say you're a wise one, but you haven't connected with the land in some time."

Autumn gave the wisps a glare, and Tavish batted at a few of them with his paw. She nodded. "I've been busy. But yes, I'll do better."

"The land knows you well, Autumn, as do the sea and sky. That's part of the reason I've come." Laith pressed his hand firmly to the ground and encouraged Autumn to do the same. "Our people deeply connect to the earth's energy. It serves as our lifeblood, and without it, we would cease to exist. Do you feel its energy?"

A slow heartbeat pulsed under Autumn's hand and warmed to a gentle, comforting heat. "Yes, I can feel the earth's pulse, but . . . it's not strong."

"No, it's not." Laith spread his fingers apart and dug them deeper into the dirt. Concentric circles of purple shimmers appeared around his hand. Autumn thought she heard a soft purring sound seeping from the ground, and Tavish flopped down on top of it, only to roll contentedly onto his back over the shimmering ground.

"Someone recently damaged the earth's spirit by stealing from it, and many worlds have felt this damage, even across the veil." Laith turned to his aunt to confirm.

"I'm afraid your *athaie* is right. I feel it each day as I gather in these woods. Somewhere nearby the spirit has been drained, and now the ground calls out a warning." Freya paused and walked toward a berry bush to pluck a few plump dark berries from a branch. Holding them in her hand, she reached them toward Autumn. "What do they tell you?"

Autumn stood to get closer to the berries. "The boundary of the earth plane has blurred."

"We know something continues to pierce it and draw on the spirit world, but we do not know how or why." Laith put his hands on Autumn's shoulders. "Your energy crosses lands. Fae, witches, and elements alike will look to you throughout time. Use the ancestors but also your inner guidance to find the cause, and remember that worlds only open if the proper connections exist."

Nodding, Autumn embraced her father and then her great-aunt. "I will, but how do I contact you again if I need you?"

Freya smiled. "I will show you how to call across worlds using the sacred tree. You are, after all, a dream walker like your mother and father. There are no lands you cannot reach."

Shaking her head in dissent, Autumn replied, "I'm not a dream walker. I've heard things of my mother, but I've never—"

"Autumn, you are many things that you may still be unaware of, and a dream walker is one of them. In time you will learn of all your gifts. The dream walking has lain dormant inside of you just as many other things still are, but you can cross worlds. Soon you will see that time, space, and worlds have no relevance to the fae, nor to you as one of us."

"I guess I'll discover it all with time." Autumn picked up the cat and snuggled him under her arm. "I need to head back, but I promise I'll connect with the earth and follow my inner guidance as well."

Laith touched Autumn's arm gently. "The ancestors' guidance comes in many forms. Be open to everything, including what lies within your own heart." He nodded to Freya before heading to the hawthorn tree. "Take care of her."

"I always do," Freya replied. "Be well, nephew, and tell my sister, Mabel, I intend to return home soon."

With a wave of his hand, Laith sent shimmers of purple lights raining down onto the mushrooms below him as he walked toward the sacred tree and disappeared into its aura.

Chapter 9

The sun had just pierced the clouds the next morning, and Autumn yawned as she followed her mother on the grass path up to the half-burned university science lab. Even this early, the open part of the building bustled with life as faculty and students scurried around to begin a new day.

On the closed section to their right, Autumn noted the extent of the fire damage. The charred section sat with drooping black beams, blown-out windows, and debris strewn everywhere. From what Autumn could see as they walked across the grass, a plastic curtain barricaded off the inside from the rest of the building.

Autumn continued following her mother and saw a woman with long strawberry-blonde hair waving in front of them. "Is that her?" Autumn questioned.

Penny nodded and waved back. "Yes, there she is."

The two of them approached the woman, who gave Penny a warm embrace and a rather large smile.

"Penny, it's been far too long!" Standing back to look at Penny, the woman shook her head as her long locks swayed with it. "I'm so glad you called me!" She had the wrinkles of a life well-lived, and yet the woman's natural beauty seemed endless.

"Autumn, this is my dear friend, Willamina Forrester." Penny placed her hand on Willamina's elbow to present her to Autumn. "She's the chair of the science department, and she's been gracious enough to walk around with us this morning and chat."

Smiling softly now, Willamina nodded. "Your mother and I go way back to our own days in the lab as students here. Of course, she focused on herbal medicine, and my courses were in biochemistry." She turned to lead the way inside the building and retrieved a badge pinned to the hip of her skirt to scan at the entry door. "I was sad to see her leave years ago, but I understood her path led in a different direction." Willamina propped the door open for them to enter. "Please."

"Thank you, Willa." Penny guided Autumn to go ahead of her, and they waited for Willa to come in behind them. "I really have missed being in the lab, but you're right. My path led me elsewhere." Penny smiled as she glanced around the building entryway. "It changed quite a bit since I was here last."

"Oh, yes! Let me show you around inside a bit." Willa led them through the entry where skylights lined the ceiling and floor-to-ceiling glass with thin mullions encased the lobby. "We had this entry done a few years ago with the endowment funds. Plus, the auditorium in the back got newly renovated as well. It's part of a showpiece approach we're taking for alumni and potential new students." She continued taking them down a narrowing hallway beside the glass exterior wall on the right and a line of windowed laboratories on the left.

"This is a beautiful space." Penny felt the pangs of nostalgia hitting her as she walked. "In many ways, it feels new, but in others, it's very much the same."

Willa grabbed at Penny's hand and gave her a tight-lipped smile. "Just say the word, and I'll speak to the herbal medicine department about having you back."

"No, Willamina, that time has passed for me. But we would appreciate having a glance at one or two of the labs and chatting with you for a while." Penny peered into the windows of a lab, watching as a few students poured substances into beakers and test tubes.

"Yes, of course. I have about an hour before my schedule begins for the day." Willa lifted her hand to direct them down the hallway. "Here, let's go to the lab at the end, shall we? Then, you can also peek into the damaged section before we go outside."

Autumn stared into the windows of the last laboratory as Willa swiped her badge at the door. "Willa, what kind of lab is this?" She watched a man roughly in his mid-twenties, who looked vaguely familiar, standing at the back of the room. He turned on a flame at the bottom of a large beaker before moving aside to gather materials. Sparks like tiny firecrackers went off inside the beaker as Autumn watched, curious as to whether some kind of unfamiliar magic played a role.

"This is the second of our chemistry labs. The primary one sat right beside this one on the end, and that was the one that sadly burned." Willa shook her head with regret. "Fortunately, the researchers and students still use this lab while we clean up from the fire. It's a bit cramped now, but we're making due."

The man at the back eyed Autumn with a stoic face. He tipped his head down to check the beaker as it flicked with firecracker sparks, and then he shot his eyes back up to her. Immediately, he turned down the flame, and the crackling stopped.

"Come!" Willa propped the lab door open again. "Let's sit outside and soak in the fresh morning air while we chat."

Penny nodded and followed her friend out to the hallway. "Yes, that sounds nice. Autumn, are you coming?" She turned to ensure that Autumn followed.

"Yeah, I'm here." Glancing back into the lab as she closed the door behind her, Autumn took one more look at the man in the lab. He looked up at her with dark eyes for a moment and then turned away. She stepped out and hurried to follow Penny and Willa. "Sorry, I'm right behind you."

They pushed their way out a side door in the glass hallway and came out onto the front lawn of the building once more. Willa made her way to a long wooden bench nestled into several bushes and flowers against the building. She patted the bench as she sat.

"Now then, tell me what's on both of your minds." Willa looked at them patiently, as if she had all the time in the world, when really, she had a tight schedule to keep.

"Willamina." Penny kept her voice down so only the three of them could hear the conversation in the tiny side garden in which they sat. "I'm sure you've heard that we discovered Autumn as our new four-points witch. As such, several duties have fallen to her, including some of the . . . unusual happenings as of late."

"I heard the news of Autumn." Willa leaned forward on the bench to smile at her around Penny, sitting between them. "That really is wonderful, and we so appreciate you leading the lot of us witches. As for her duties, I'm afraid I'm unaware of what's been happening, really. I've been so focused on my position as chair here in the department that I haven't had time to take the pulse on the outside community. Tell me, what is it I can help with?"

"We suspect some ill will behind the lab fire and possibly some magical workings going on as well." Autumn tilted her head apologetically. "I don't mean to bring unnecessary stress on you, but there seems to be something going on in the department that led to Rowan Stewart's death in the fire."

"Oh, that poor girl." Willa stroked her lip with her fingertips as she thought for a moment. "I don't know why she came to the lab that day, but the researchers take every opportunity to work on their projects. As far as magic in the laboratories, I can tell you we have quite a few witches working here, but Rowan wasn't one of them. Perhaps someone got careless, and she caught a glimpse of magic that was otherwise meant to be hidden."

Autumn wrapped her hands around her crossed legs and leaned back. "But do people use their magic to support their research? Is that allowed?"

"Good heavens, no." Willamina crossed her legs and shook her bohemian skirt out until it was loose around her. "Well, at least, not where proper science is concerned. We do not want to affect our research through our own wills. However, since magic inherently lies within us witches, it comes through in all we do. We cannot deny that, but we must be aware of its impact on our studies and take steps to contain it as best we can."

"I understand, but I sense magic at work here . . . even if trying to be held back." Autumn looked around the grassy area surrounding them. "It worries me that maybe someone intended for it to do damage, though."

Willa raised her chin toward the parking lot. "I don't know about intentional magic being done under the surface. However, I can point you to the one the department's keeping an eye on after the arson. He's the chemistry lab manager, Callum, and he is also, in fact, a witch. You can see him walking into the building now."

Autumn and Penny both turned their heads at once to the grass walkway leading to the front entry. Hurrying toward the building with his head down, ear-length black hair covering his face, Callum carried a sweating to-go cup from The Mountain Juicery with what appeared to be a yellow drink inside. In his other hand, he gripped a black binder with an upside-down black triangle and a line drawn straight through it on the cover. Autumn recognized it instantly as the symbol for earth. A gray messenger bag ran across his shoulder and offset his all-black clothes. Autumn noticed a few glimmers of green shimmering from the edge of the bag.

"Is he an earth witch?" Autumn watched him intently as he waited until someone held the door open before he disappeared into the building.

"Yes, I believe so," Willa confirmed. "His studies revolve around forest fire mitigation efforts, and he uses samples from the woods to test in the lab. From what I've heard around the department, the police have been looking into him for the arson. He claimed he lost his access card, but otherwise as the lab manager, he had free rein to the lab and apparently no alibi. Although, from my perspective, I have no idea why he'd set fire to the department when his grant money is up for review again. It just doesn't make sense to bite the hand that feeds you, if you ask me."

As Autumn considered Willa's words, her eyes drifted around the scene. She noticed students still trickling in for their morning classes, some on foot and others by bike. One student chained up their bike on a long rack that lined a sidewalk to the side entrance. Autumn focused on the bike directly beside that one.

The black mountain bike sat on the very end of the rack, with its front tire strewn over it. Stickers plastered the center bar of the frame, some for mountain-region bike races and a few with hand-drawn symbols, looking strikingly similar to the style of symbols the girls had discovered in Rowan's apartment.

Autumn's mouth dropped open as she stood up to get a closer look at the bike. She looked around her to see if anyone was watching, and then she pulled out her phone to snap a picture of the symbols. Bending down, she ran her hand along a drawing of a circle with an arrow sticking out to the right.

Just as her fingers touched the symbol, the wind picked up around her, sweeping her hair up with it. Her gran's necklace felt warm beneath her collar, and she pressed her hand firmly against her chest to absorb the heat. Then, she felt the whispers of the ancestors forming on the wind.

"Follow the symbols to a deeper pain."

The symbols felt hot under her fingertips, and Autumn pulled back from the bike to stand. She panted as she stared off into the grass in front of her. Then, the vision of the photo in Rowan's apartment came to her. The man she had just seen inside the chemistry lab was Rowan's ex-boyfriend from the photo, and he owned this mountain bike.

"Autumn, are you all right?" her mother called.

Autumn shook her head and turned, still pressing one hand to Gran's necklace under her collar. "Yeah, I think so. I just . . ."

"Oh, dear. Your gran's necklace." Penny stood and walked over to her daughter. "What shall we do?"

Willamina stared at them both with concern and waited for a moment. "Is there something to be concerned about?"

Removing her hand and resuming a calm demeanor, Autumn smiled. "No, everything is all right. Thank you for the tour and the information, Willamina. Can we contact you again if anything comes up?"

"Yes, please do. Your mother has my number, and I'm more than willing to help. Anything to keep the energy balance." Willamina took Penny's hands in hers and patted them. "It was good to see you, my friend. You know where to find me."

"I do." With a wave, Penny took Autumn's elbow, and they walked toward the parking lot, leaving Willamina to her schedule.

After the two of them stood out of earshot, Penny leaned into Autumn. "What did you hear?"

"The ancestors . . ." Relief washed over Autumn for a moment as she thanked the ancestors in her mind for returning with guidance. "Something about following the symbols to a deeper pain. Those markings hold the key. I can feel it, but I still don't know the right questions to ask. Although, I am glad the ancestors have come back to me." Autumn hopped into her mother's old Range Rover, and they started backing away. "For a while after Ayla Ross's disappearance, something inside me wanted this all to stop, and I think I unconsciously pushed their guidance to the side. It was too much to deal with, but now . . . I want to help Anabeth understand her cousin's death. It feels close, almost like what I went through when Gran died."

Her mother nodded as she drove them away from the university. "I can understand that, dear, but you cannot deny who you are."

"No, I don't want to. I want to know more of who I am, witch and fae. And I welcome back the ancestors' voices for as long as they're willing to remain." Autumn fiddled with her gran's necklace as she spoke. "Yet something tells me they won't."

Penny reached her right hand out to brush a strand of hair from Autumn's face. "We connect with the energies that support us for our highest good. If the ancestors' time with you is limited, then perhaps it's as it should be. I doubt they will ever leave your side, even if you can no longer hear their whispers."

Autumn nodded and tilted her head back on the headrest. "You're right, Mom. I'm grateful for their guidance now."

Penny gave a resolute head nod. "Good. So what's the next step?"

"We need to find out more about this fire because we still have two suspects wandering around the building. Willa mentioned Callum, the lab manager, and I also saw Rowan's ex-boyfriend Keith inside. I bet at least one of them knows exactly what's going on and may even be at fault."

"It sounds like we should pay a visit to the fire chief. Would you like to notify the mayor that we're going to see his brother?"

Autumn pulled out her phone and nodded. "Sure, but as far as I can remember, the mayor has recurring meetings all day on Mondays. So before we do that, how does a cold drink sound? That new juice bar, The Mountain Juicery, opened a few months ago, and I haven't made it over there yet. Wanna grab something?"

Penny looked curiously at her daughter. "That sounds nice, but do we have time for all of this, or will the shop overwhelm Simone by herself?"

Pausing for a moment to receive insight, Autumn knew Simone had an empty shop to herself while she cranked up Joan Jett in the background and worked on new paper patterns. "Simone's good. She's got a quiet shop, and she's happy. But I for one could use a mango juice."

"Mango juice, huh?" Penny raised an eyebrow at her daughter. "Does this have anything to do with this case?"

Laughing under her breath, Autumn replied, "Always. So let's go see a barista about an ice cold juice and a dark-haired earth witch who may also have a thing for mango."

Chapter 10

The new juicery sat on the end of Main Street across from the Book Nook and several blocks down from Parchment and Pine. The shop's A-frame sign promoted the recent opening at the curb and beckoned students, locals, and visitors with an offer for a second juice at twenty percent off.

Penny gathered her satchel from the back seat of the Range Rover just as her phone buzzed furiously at her. "My, oh my. This phone sure wants my attention! Let's see." She pulled out the dated flip phone she couldn't seem to part with and answered.

Autumn eyed her mother curiously as she spoke to someone on the other end. When Penny hung up, Autumn slammed the car door and gave her mother a look. "What's going on, Mom?"

Penny sighed. "Well, Vera Cunningham has an awful case of allergies, and she needs some healing teas ASAP." She pressed a few buttons on the keypad and listened to another message. "And Mayor Halpin appears to be on the same wavelength as us. Simone says his office called your shop asking you to meet at the fire station this afternoon. You must have known he had it in his mind to call."

"Hmm, yeah, I guess he popped into my mind as we were thinking about the fire. Okay, I'll grab Simone this afternoon before heading over there." Autumn gathered her things at her feet. "Do you need to go to Vera's right away, or can you grab that juice with me?"

Shaking her head, Penny stuffed her phone back into her bag and threw it in the back seat. "No, I'm afraid being the new town tea lady has its obligations. I'll go right over and help Vera. Will you be all right by yourself?"

Autumn waved a hand through the air. "Oh, yeah. I'll just see if they remember our lab friend. Maybe I can bring out that air energy charisma and charm them into giving me some info."

Penny laughed at her daughter. "Just be wise about it, whatever you do. This small town talks. And while they may talk to you, they'll also talk to others, too."

"I know, Mom. I'm always careful how I approach things." Autumn stepped away from the curb. "Tell Vera I said hello."

Waving at her, Penny drove off toward Crescent House. Autumn faced The Mountain Juicery behind her. Large wooden crates sat stacked in the window, with piles of lemons, oranges, and apples filling them. Fairy lights hung from the ceiling, along with black pendant lights and greenery.

She pulled the door open to the shop and stepped inside, looking around for a moment. On her right, sitting at a small table with his laptop, Finn watched the baristas working. She smiled and walked over.

"Hello again." Autumn pointed to his laptop. "Hard at work?"

"Autumn, uh . . . kind of." Finn pulled out a chair for her to sit. He lowered his voice a bit. "I'm observing, actually. Turns out, people consider this the new summer hangout for the university, especially for poor grad students stuck here doing research over the summer with no money and no time to eat." He raised his eyebrows at her. "I thought I'd sit here and see if anything comes up about the fire."

"Well, what've you heard so far?" Autumn threw her backpack onto the chair beside her and pulled out her wallet.

"The usual gossip about the dean with a student, computers being hacked, and a solstice party at the frat houses." He tilted his head at her. "But really . . . people know that the fire's being considered arson now, and they're speculating about who did it and why. Most people are gone for the summer now, you know? So there's really only a small amount of finger-pointing that people can do, and it's all pointing to some guy who runs the lab."

"Callum . . . McIver, I believe. I saw him this morning at the lab, and he's definitely a suspect." Autumn watched as Finn typed the name on his laptop keys as tiny golden shimmers flew off his fingertips.

"What did you make of him?" Finn looked up, waiting for Autumn's reply.

She shrugged. "Dark and introverted. He kept his head down to avoid all the attention, but I noticed a couple things. For one, he had an earth symbol on his notebook, and the department chair confirmed that he's an earth witch. Apparently he does some sort of research on fire mitigation, so there's a connection there. He also needs grant money to maintain his research."

"So that's the second guy in Rowan's life who needed money, huh?" Finn typed a bit more while he thought.

"Yep, and apparently he's one of the grad students who frequents this place, because he had a juice in hand as he walked into the lab." She leaned in a little closer to whisper. "In fact, I'm hoping to get some info about him from the barista somehow."

Finn looked up from his keyboard and nodded as he thought. "You need a drink. Come on, just follow my lead."

He stood and made his way up to the counter. Autumn hesitated and then followed.

"I'll wait with you while you order," he said.

"Oh, okay." Autumn squinted at him for a moment, wondering what he was up to. Then, she glanced at the menu quickly before a barista came up to the cash register.

"Welcome to The Mountain Juicery. What can I get for you?" A girl with shoulder-length bleach-blonde hair looked at Autumn as she waited to press the keys on the register.

"Uh, hi. I'll have a pineapple mango dream, please." Autumn smiled and gave her the payment.

"Hey," Finn interjected. "Didn't you bump into someone here the other day and mix up your research papers?"

Autumn stared at him blankly, and the barista looked up to do the same.

"You said you thought it was some dark and strangely introverted guy, right?" Finn widened his eyes at Autumn to play along, and she caught a few glimmers of magic in his eyes.

She nodded and turned back to the barista. "Right, yeah. I did." Pausing for a moment to decipher how best to connect with the girl, Autumn continued. "My advisor won't be happy that I just lost an entire week's worth of findings. I really need to get those papers back."

The girl grabbed the printed receipt from the top of the register and gave it to Autumn. "Well, I think I know the guy you're talking about. I mean, I totally understand being on the bad side of your advisor, so if you want your papers back, that guy's here every day."

"Oh, really?" Autumn perked up at her openness.

"Yeah, dark-black hair to his ears. Wears black and doesn't want to have a conversation?" She walked toward the back counter to make Autumn's juice as they talked.

"That sounds like him, yeah." Autumn leaned against the glass juice counter full of fruits and vegetables as she waited for more information.

"From what I can tell, he goes to his lab early and spends the entire day there. Sometimes he even comes in at the end of the day, too. But he's always messing with some binder he carries around while he orders his juice with lots of ice. Something about working in a hot environment." She shrugged. "I don't know, but I'm sure he'll be in again tomorrow morning and the next day. I can pretty much guarantee he'll come in for his usual super-icy juice and keep to himself on the way out." She handed a tall yellow to-go cup to Autumn over the top of the counter. "Here's your dream."

Smiling, Autumn took the cup and gave her a wave. "Thanks a lot!"

"Yeah, no problem." The girl returned to the register to serve some other students who had walked in.

As Autumn pulled the chair out at Finn's table, she slurped on her juice. "Oh, this is really good! Did you get some?"

"Nah, I just grabbed a banana. I'm more of a coffee guy myself." He typed away at his laptop and then leaned in. "So do you wanna come back and scope him out tomorrow?"

Autumn pulled at the straw in her juice cup, thinking. "I don't think we need to." She couldn't put her finger on why this juice place might be important, but she could feel it. "There's something about him and this place, though. She said he comes in every morning for an icy drink because he's working somewhere hot all day. It's possible he's working with fire, even outside of his research."

Finn crossed his arms and nodded. "Makes sense to balance out the heat of some alchemical experiments with a little daily dose of icy fruit."

Picking up her cup again to take a sip, Autumn slid her hand down the sweating sides. Her eyes wandered to the sweat ring that formed on the table where it had just sat. She stared around at the other tables as well, and most had similar surface stains.

"What're you thinking?" Finn squinted at her before a group of loud students heading out the door distracted him.

Autumn shook off her thoughts. "Oh, it's nothing."

He leaned over the table toward her. "The little things are infinitely the most important."

She smiled. "What?"

"Sir Arthur Conan Doyle in Sherlock Holmes." He lifted a hand as if to ask if she really didn't know what he was saying. "It's always the little things, so don't dismiss whatever catches your attention."

Autumn scoffed. "Right, no, I know. I was just thinking that it's summer, and the heat is getting to everyone, that's all." She leaned in closer. "Anyway, I forgot to ask about Anabeth. How is she?"

"Back at it. She's on another story right now, but every chance she gets she checks in with me about Rowan's case." Finn closed up his laptop and started packing his messenger bag.

"Is she still shaken over the attempted break-in?" Autumn stood and sipped her juice while watching Finn pack up.

"If she is, she doesn't let on. You know how she tries to act like nothing gets to her." He started toward the door and held it open for Autumn. "But listen, Autumn. My aunt told me you spoke to her . . . about the elder."

They stopped out on the sidewalk, and both glanced quickly around them to ensure no one stood within earshot.

"He's one of the oldest practicing alchemists in the witch community. A hedge witch of sorts, and his specialty lies in dissolution. Finding the parts of ourselves hidden in the unconscious, especially those tied to our fate." Finn rubbed the back of his neck as he continued. "Although he may have the answers that you need to solve this case, he also may show you who you truly are."

Autumn pushed her hands down into the pockets of her baggy linen pants and rocked back on her heels. "So, is this a warning?"

"I just want you to be prepared for whatever you find there. For this case or for yourself." Finn headed to a wrought-iron bench nearby and pulled out a key to unlock a bicycle chained to it. "I visited him once as a child with my aunt, and while on his property, I saw the path leading me back to Hollow's

Glenn, but . . . even with fate, it takes inner work to get to the proper place."

"Okay, so the elder is a hedge witch. Got it." A vision flashed in Autumn's mind of a cave with ancient symbols carved around the exterior doorway. With another flash, she saw a grassy path leading toward distant standing stones.

As a car horn sounded on the street beside them, she regained awareness and focused on Finn, getting onto his bicycle.

She thought about the carved symbols in her mind's eye. "Your aunt said we needed to ask the right questions. How do I do that?"

Finn flipped one of the bike pedals into position with his right foot and pressed down into it. "Everything in alchemy derives from a formula. Find the pieces of the formula, and then you speak his language."

Nodding, Autumn repeated his words. "A formula. Find the formula." And with a quick salute, Finn headed off into the distance of the swirling cerulean-tinted air lining Main Street, hinting at something beyond their comprehension.

Chapter 11

Tavish trotted up to Autumn immediately upon her arrival and brushed against her legs. Autumn threw her backpack over a hook at the front of Parchment and Pine and bent down to give the cat a much-appreciated head scratch.

"Hey, little guy. I missed you this morning, too." She smiled, grabbed the handful of mail that she brought in with her, and made her way to the back of the shop.

Simone peeked her head out from behind the computer at the back counter. "It's been slow today, so I'm just making patterns for next season's collection."

Nodding, Autumn came around the back of the counter. "I figured. That's why I left you for a while. I know you like it when no one's around to disturb you."

"Yeah, well, the phone still rang off the hook. Did Aunt Penny tell you the mayor's office called?" Simone put the computer to sleep and tucked her legs up to her chest on her chair.

"She said the mayor wants to meet us at the fire station this afternoon. I was planning to ask him to meet us over there anyway, but I guess they're saving me the trouble." Autumn flipped the mail and lifted a bright-yellow envelope up for Simone to see. "I bet this is the chamber of commerce reminding us to decorate the shop for the Sun Day Shopping solstice event. Marion Bennett mentioned it at the last preservation meeting." She opened the envelope and read it aloud. "Encourage Main Street shoppers with our summer Sun Day Shopping event. Decorate your shop with solstice-themed decor that welcomes customers for a full day of shopping with longer sunlight. We also encourage you to host special sales that day to attract attention. The best decorated shop wins a prize."

"Why is it always about the sun? This makes no sense to me every year. The solstice means welcoming in the darker days to come, not just celebrating the sun. Let's have a little moon magic for once." Simone huffed as she walked to the back room and turned off the overhead music. "It really bugs me. Do we have to participate?"

"Yes, we do, so quit being a downer about it. You know you love the solstice, and we'll get to celebrate the dark at home with the family, right, Tav?" Autumn patted her hip, and Tavish showed up beneath her for more attention.

"Anyway, we need to head over to the fire station. I bet they're waiting for us now. Grab the lights?" Simone pulled her black over-the-shoulder tote bag out from under the counter and headed toward the front door.

"All right, I'm coming." Autumn looked down at the cat as she flipped the lights. "Tav, we'll be back for you soon. Just curl up in the hearth room, okay?" He meowed back at her and trotted over to rub against the thick curtains that lined the hearth room. "There you go. Be good."

Simone held the front door open and flipped the sign to Closed. With a good yank of the antique handle, she locked the door behind them both. "Let's just hop into the SUV and head over there. I can feel the mayor's anxiousness from here." She pointed to her car sitting on the curb in front of the flower shop next door.

"Planning ahead, I see." Autumn got into the SUV and received a download as she put her bag on the floor. "Lainy's there, too. There's something they want to show us."

Squinting as she started the car and drove away, Simone gave her cousin a sideways stare. "From the fire?"

"I'm not sure, exactly, but it must be. Why else would they call us over to the fire station with Lainy?" Autumn put a hand over Gran's locket at her chest. She closed her eyes and called to the ancestors. "Guide us, ancestors. Allow me to hear your calls, and I will answer with my gifts."

"Everything okay?" Simone drove a few blocks down toward the city hall square, and Autumn stared off toward the bell tower that had brought her pain just a few months back.

"Yeah, I'm just taking some advice to connect more deeply with the ancestors and get to know more of who I am." Autumn shook off the daze and smiled at her cousin before trailing her eyes over to the bell tower again.

"But you're good, right?" Simone parked the car in a corner spot behind the fire station and put a hand on Autumn's forearm. "You're not gonna keel over on me anymore?"

Autumn laughed and shook her head. "No, Sim. I'm good. I haven't felt any weakness around the bell in a while now. It's just that I still have concerns about my connection with the ancestors. While I have heard their voices recently, they seem distant when I hear them. I do, however, keep having more visions than ever before." They hopped out of the car and headed toward the station door. "Maybe things need to change, like you said. This might relate to all the big shifts in my gifts since becoming the four-points witch."

Simone chuckled under her breath. "Tell me about it. If mermaid scales are any sign of how I've changed since we started this four-points coven, then I'd say I'm right there with you on the weirdness factor."

As they pulled the side door open to the large truck bay, Lainy stood there with relief. "There you are! We've been waiting, and it sounds like this could be a head-scratcher."

Simone and Autumn exchanged curious glances before Mayor Halpin, Chief Walsh, Officer Ben Walsh, and Fire Chief Halpin all trickled out of the corner office.

"Ah, Autumn, Simone! You made it!" the mayor announced. "I'm sorry my office called you over abruptly, but well, you know the nature of things." He cleared his throat and lifted his hand to present everyone beside him. "I brought Lainy along with me from city hall. Chief Walsh brought Ben with him today since I suspect the latest votes will put him as the clear winner to take over as police chief soon. And I'm not sure if you've met my brother, Ardie Halpin, but he's the fire chief here."

Autumn and Simone moved forward to shake Fire Chief Halpin's hand. "Hello, Chief Halpin. It's nice to meet you finally," Autumn said with a warm smile.

"Oh, the pleasure's all mine, Ms. MacKinnon. I've heard a great deal of things about you and your cousin here, and I appreciate all you've done for the mountain region." The fire chief gave her a nod and then stepped back into line with the rest of them.

Simone glanced over to Ben, and he gave her a wink, whispering under his breath, "Hi." She smirked before drawing her attention back to the mayor.

"Now, then. I think it's best we move into the office to speak, don't you, Ardie?" The mayor moved aside for his brother to lead the way down a small corridor to a large corner office. "Thank you, Ardie. Gather in, all of you, please."

They moved into a substantially sized office with a dark oak desk sitting in front of a glass picture window. The office overlooked a side garden of city hall square with abundant trees and benches lining small squares of grass. People walked in the distance toward city hall and the police station, but the garden outside the office was nestled into the corner, nicely out of plain sight.

Each of them found a seat on large, cushioned sofas and a few chairs that lined the room. The fire chief swiveled around in his desk chair to gather documents and photos and lay them out in front of them.

"Right, then," Mayor Halpin started. "As you all know, our investigators deemed the fire at the university laboratory to be arson. I'll let Ardie explain, but to be clear, we don't know if this situation involves magic or something similar, and we need all of your help to determine what's going on. Ardie?"

"Thank you, Stephen." Chief Halpin stood from his desk chair and tapped his finger over a few photos he'd laid out on his desk. "Our fire investigation team took these photos at the scene. The entire back half of the laboratory exploded in the fire, and a substantial amount of chemicals permeated the air as we arrived. Of course, that's expected for a science lab, but there were some disturbing findings." He talked with his hands as he described the scene. "For one, the amount of sulfur in the air sat at extremely high levels, more than we'd expect for typical experiments. We needed to use our chem gear and take extra precautions when we arrived on the scene. I even called Chief Walsh's explosive ordinance team to be sure we had our bases covered if the entire place went up, but thankfully that didn't happen."

Chief Walsh nodded and leaned over to rest his forearms on his knees as he peered at the photos. "I'm just glad nothing came of it, but we're always here to help."

"Now, my fire investigator found the origin of the fire at this point here." Chief Halpin pointed to an image of a black-topped lab counter with a large ring of bubbled material melted through the top of it. "The resin of the counter melted away, and a bubbling ring of silver liquid formed around the ring, along with this." He pointed to another image of what looked like burning red lava rock. "We're sending it to the forensics lab now, along with the silver, which we assume is mercury."

"Lava rock and quicksilver?" Chief Walsh turned to his son, Ben, across from him. "How in the world would someone get those around here? And why?"

"They weren't part of the experiments being done in the chemistry lab for research?" Autumn questioned.

Chief Halpin shook his head. "We checked with the department about all their current research, and not one of them includes anything like this."

"That's not the strangest part, though," the mayor interjected, and stepped up to sort through the photos on the desk. He picked one from the bottom and pulled it to the top, tapping his finger on it for emphasis. "Talk about this one, please, Ardie?"

"Yes, well, this really is peculiar." He ran his pointer along a section of the photo showing the ceiling. "If you look closely, you can see that all the materials in the building appear to have rotted away. Usually, we see black soot over everything, twisted and melted metal, and deterioration. But this . . . It's as if the building sat in a damp rainforest for thousands of years."

Autumn stepped up to the desk and eyed the images closely. All the surfaces in the burned building had a rotted appearance, like the surface of a shriveled, moldy pumpkin sitting in the sun weeks after Samhain.

"And the stench in the air . . . It wasn't just the overpowering, toxic scent of sulfur." The fire chief shook his head as he glanced over the images. "It was putrid. Not smoky from a typical explosion, but putrid as if it was a rotting pit of fermenting matter. I've never experienced anything like it."

"Lainy?" The mayor put his hand on Lainy's shoulder beside him. "You're a fire witch just as my brother and I are. What do you make of this?"

Lainy stood up and made her way over to the desk to peruse the images next. Shaking her head, she lifted her eyes. "I have no idea, Mr. Mayor. I've spent many years wielding fire and becoming one with it, but this appears new to me as well."

"But could it be magical workings, though? That is the question at hand." Mayor Halpin looked to Autumn now. "Autumn, do you have any insights?"

Autumn shrugged and stared blankly at them all. "I don't see any indication of magic. Chief, did anyone notice any shimmers at the scene?"

"Not that I'm aware of, no." Chief Halpin rubbed his scruffy bearded chin. "I can't put my finger on it, but something about this fire isn't normal."

Autumn and Simone exchanged knowing glances. "Alchemy," Autumn said bluntly. "The fire must have something to do with ancient alchemy. Chief Walsh, we've been looking into the girl who died in the fire, Rowan Stewart. Apparently she had concerns about unexplained magic in the lab, and she sent some pictures of alchemical formulas to her cousin, Anabeth, before she died. It's gotta be connected somehow."

"Ben, let's have another chat with Anabeth and see what comes up," Chief Walsh confirmed with his son. "We're continuing to investigate Rowan's connection with the arson as well, Autumn. In fact . . ." He trailed off as he watched Autumn stare into the distance for a minute. "Autumn?"

Simone nudged her cousin to jerk her out of her daze. "Cuz, are you okay?"

"Um." Autumn blinked a few times and eyed Chief Halpin for a minute. She caught a vision of some large chemical bottles, and something told her to ask about the fire inspector.

"Actually, sorry, everyone. Chief Halpin, could you show me the fire investigator's materials? Maybe where he works?"

"Of course." The fire chief made his way around the desk and to the door.

Autumn put a hand on Chief Walsh's arm. "Sorry to cut you off, Chief. I promise to let you finish, but something's drawing my attention."

"No worries, Autumn. We'll get to it. You just follow your instincts and lead the way." Chief Walsh trailed behind her as she proceeded into the hallway toward a locker room filled with equipment.

Red metal grate lockers lined both sides of the room, and each bore a firefighter's name at the top. At the end of the row, Chief Halpin stood beside a much larger locker that read Carson.

"This one here belongs to my fire inspector, Alick Carson. He's got chemicals, tools, and equipment he needs for fire forensics in here. Then, this one beside it houses his personal equipment." The chief stretched a long-wired keychain from the side of his belt and pulled out a key to unlock both lockers.

Autumn moved forward and ran a hand across the contents of the chemical jars as the others watched her curiously. On a shelf sat several binders filled with hazardous material sheets. A box full of dark-brown tincture jars labeled Iodine rattled around as she moved things around in the locker. She proceeded to Alick's personal locker and opened the door.

Upon moving a hanging shirt out of the way, Autumn stopped as she spotted a picture clipped to the side of the locker. She pulled it from the clip and raised it for the others to see. Pointing to a girl in the photo, Autumn swallowed hard. "This is Rowan Stewart, the girl who died in the lab fire."

Ben stepped forward and took the photo from Autumn. Nodding, he gave the photo to his father. "She's right, Chief. It's the same girl."

Chief Walsh inspected it as he rubbed the back of his neck. He eyed the man holding Rowan on his lap, arms wrapped around her in the photo. "Ardie, did you know Alick was seeing this girl Rowan?" He looked over at Chief Halpin beside him.

"I don't think he was still seeing her, but I'm pretty sure he was in love with her." Everyone's wide eyes fell on the chief, and he stumbled back a step in surprise. "Whoa, don't all jump on this at once! From what I know, they met sometime within the past year, but he had several years on her. Plus, she had been involved with another fellow who was no good for her. She kept going back to him over Alick, for some reason. Word around the station was that Alick wanted her to leave that other fellow for good and go away with him." Chief Halpin shook his head and eyed the name tape on the locker. "I've known Alick for decades, though. He would never leave this job or Hollow's Glenn. He's married to the fire. It's in him just as it's in us, and I doubt a girl could keep him away."

"But he wanted her to leave the other guy?" Simone chimed in. "Must have been the ex-boyfriend Keith that Anabeth mentioned. He sounded like a real charmer."

Chief Walsh cleared his throat. "Autumn, can I have a word?" He tilted his head to the side to lead her away from the others. He waved his hand for Ben to come along with them. "About what I intended to say back in the office . . . You must have sensed something out here connected, because we found correspondence on Rowan's computer. Right, Ben?"

Ben nodded. "That's right. Some messages came from an unknown lover urging her to move in with him. Hearing the fire chief, I'm assuming now that those came from Alick Carson. And there were other concerning messages with a more threatening tone. It seems Rowan found out someone hacked into the university computer system to not only access secure research findings but also funnel money out of department accounts. She reported it all to the department, but someone sent a few threatening emails to her afterward. We don't know what's connected right now, but as far as we can tell, Rowan sure seems like the target of the fire. And now that Alick has her picture plastered all over his locker beside a lot of fire chemicals . . ."

"This doesn't look good for him at all." Autumn turned back to look at the lockers full of chemicals.

"No, it doesn't," Chief Walsh replied.

"Although, if he loved Rowan, why try to kill her?" Autumn paused to receive any insight that would come. "Maybe she didn't wanna leave her ex for him, but still. Something doesn't feel right."

"We'll deal with Alick to determine his connection. The other one we're looking into is the lab manager." Ben kept his voice quiet so only the three of them would hear.

"Callum McIver," Autumn replied.

"That's right." Ben gave her a serious look. "We know he's a witch, Autumn, so you've gotta let us in on anything you may know about him."

She shrugged and sighed. "I don't know much . . . yet. But I intend to find out. He is a witch, but there's more to this than elemental magic. That works with the flow of nature, and this fire feels more like forces meddling in an unnatural way. I'm not sure how else to describe it, but I'll let you know if I discover anything more."

The chief looped his thumbs through the top of his belt and nodded. "All right, then." He headed back over to the group and shook hands with Chief Halpin. "Thank you for your time today, Ardie. I'm sorry to see you on such an unfortunate occasion, but nonetheless, it's good to see you."

"Likewise, Ian. Keep me updated on what you find about the fire." Chief Halpin patted him on the back.

Mayor Halpin stepped up to shake Chief Walsh's hand, along with Ben's. "Call my office if there's anything you need. And as always, Ian, please keep Autumn in the loop as well. If this last year gave us any indication, Hollow's Glenn needs her gifts now more than ever . . . And that of the entire coven. I don't know where we'd be without them."

"Let me walk you all out," Chief Halpin suggested. He pushed open a side door leading back into the truck bay where the fire engines sat.

A few firefighters worked on an engine as the group of them passed by and smiled. Autumn noted the powerful scent of fennel throughout the bay, a symbol of courage, strength, and loyalty. If a connection existed between Alick and Rowan's death, it would be hard-fought to uncover it with a band of brothers close around him.

As she continued toward the door, Autumn's locket warmed on her chest. She stopped walking, at first wondering whether it was just a warning about Alick. Yet, her attention drew to a bulletin board covered in community news beside her. A familiar flier hung dead center with arrows drawn to specific dates.

"Chief Halpin?" Autumn stood directly in front of the board, and Simone came up beside her, sensing right away what her cousin stared at.

"Yes, Autumn? Everything all right?" The fire chief wandered back through the others as they dispersed.

"This mountain bike race that you have posted . . . Is there someone in the firehouse who'll be in the race?" Autumn caught Chief Walsh also listening by the door.

"Oh yes! One of our very own will participate, and we'll have a truck or two out at the event tomorrow just in case. Will you be there?" The chief put his hands on his hips and waited for Autumn's response.

She looked at Simone smirking beside her and then over at Chief Walsh's curious face. "Something tells me it's not something to be missed."

Chapter 12

Autumn wrapped Tavish up in a cozy flannel blanket and carried him out the back door of Parchment and Pine. Simone waited with the engine running to drive them home for the evening.

Waving her cousin into the car, Simone sighed. "I can't wait to get home for some veggie lasagna and reruns of *The X-Files*."

Laughing under her breath, Autumn slid Tavish into the back seat. "You are such a water witch, all dark and moody."

Simone smiled and took it as a compliment. "Yes, yes, I am." But as a buzzing came from Autumn's backpack, Simone's mood dampened. She clenched the steering wheel in her hands and sighed. "Whoever it is needs to leave us alone. My lasagna's waiting."

Autumn noted Anabeth's name as she pulled her phone out and got settled into the passenger seat. "Anabeth messaged me. I hope she's okay." Autumn scrolled through the message as Simone drove toward Hawthorn Cottage.

The clock on Autumn's phone read six, which still gave them a bit of time. She leaned back on the headrest and looked at Simone.

"No, I told you I'm eating lasagna and watching *The X-Files*." Simone shook her head. "You're not dragging me anywhere else tonight."

"Anabeth's family is having a memorial service for Rowan tonight, and she'd really like us to attend."

"Tonight? That's really last minute." Simone sighed. It had already been a long day fielding phone calls at the shop in addition to the fire station visit. The last thing she wanted to do was talk to a bunch of people she didn't know at the memorial service. "Do we have to go?"

Autumn raised her eyebrows. "Yes, Miss Anti-Social. We have to go. Anabeth is our friend, and we have to support her right now." She shrugged and looked out the window. "Besides, I get the idea there'll be some interactions worth seeing there."

Simone exhaled a breath that sent the dark hair framing her face flying up. "Fine, we can go, but you owe me for missing my night in." She shook her head and thought about it. "I guess

I can try on that new black jumpsuit with the deep V in the back."

"Oh, you mean the one you bought to wear for Ben?" Autumn smirked as she pulled a small brush out of her backpack and began stroking it through her long locks to get ready.

"I didn't buy it for Ben, thank you very much." Simone quickly glared at her cousin before pulling up to Hawthorn Cottage. "I bought it because I needed a new cocktail-style outfit. If I get the chance to wear it out with him, then I'll put it to good use."

"Uh, huh." Autumn grabbed Tavish, slammed the door on the SUV, and headed up to the cottage. "The memorial service starts in about an hour, so can you be ready in forty-five minutes?"

"That's the beauty of a black one-piece jumpsuit. Makes everything super simple." Simone pushed the door open for them and threw her bag down at the front. "Be out in a few."

Autumn nodded and headed to her room to get ready as well. When they both wandered back out, Autumn had dressed in a deep eggplant-colored wrap dress with her grandmother's locket at her neck. Simone wore her new jumpsuit and had clipped her short bob back with a black onyx hair comb.

"Hey, can I leave my backpack in the car and throw a few items in your pockets when we get there?" Autumn scurried around to pop on a quick shimmer of lip gloss and head to the door.

"Of course, but nothing too bulky." Simone stretched her hands into her silky pockets. "These pants aren't made for long hikes or anything."

"I suspect not." Autumn looked Simone up and down. "I love that outfit on you, though. Ben would be quite lucky to see you in it."

Simone blushed a bit. "Thanks, cuz." Turning her attention to the task at hand, she pulled the front door open for them. "Let's go."

They headed out into the evening again, driving over to an outdoor garden venue where the service was being held. A large trellis draped with green vines and fairy lights stood at the entry to the garden. Alongside it, a sign marked the occasion and directed guests into the main garden space for Rowan's memorial.

"You go ahead. I'm just gonna grab a few things out of my bag and then throw it in the trunk." Autumn grabbed the keys from Simone after they parked.

"All right, but don't leave me in there by myself for too long." Simone pointed a finger at her cousin.

Shaking her head, Autumn lifted her right hand to promise. "Never. I'll be right behind you."

Simone agreed and headed in on her own as Autumn rifled through her backpack. She pulled out a small change purse and shoved a lip gloss inside. As she grabbed the backpack to take it to the trunk, she noticed Callum McIver stopping before the entrance to the gardens.

Autumn crouched down behind the passenger side of the SUV to observe him. He was dressed in all black from head to toe and carried another smoothie to-go cup in his hand that he nervously nursed from. As he paced back and forth a bit, Autumn noticed a marking on the inside of his wrist.

It appeared to be a black upside-down triangle with a horizontal line drawn through the top section. Autumn recognized it immediately as the symbol for earth, which made sense if he was indeed an earth witch. Although elemental witches rarely displayed such symbols prominently, she recognized each witch had their own magical practice.

Callum looked through the garden archway and took a deep breath. He left his drink on a stone bench sitting beside the entry and strode in. Autumn stood up and quickly put her bag in the trunk and locked up, eager to follow him inside.

As soon as she stepped into the garden, she noticed the large photo of Rowan on an easel at the front. Bouquets of flowers sat on either side of the photo, and several people meandered up to admire the happy photo of her.

Simone wandered over and wrapped her arm through Autumn's. "Finally. I had to endure a conversation with Anabeth and Rowan's great-aunt about the fashion in her day. What took you so long?"

Autumn whispered into her ear. "Callum just walked in, and he seemed rather hesitant to attend the service."

Simone nodded and raised her chin toward a side table with refreshments. "The ex-boyfriend, Keith, made it, too. He's over there grabbing a drink, and Anabeth's not too happy about it."

The girls watched as Callum walked over to grab some water at the edge of the refreshment table. Keith spotted him on the other end, and an angry look crossed his face.

Keith approached Callum and slammed his drink down in front of him on the table, allowing it to splash up onto Callum's shirt. Callum calmly grabbed a napkin and began wiping the spill from his clothes.

"What're you doing here?" Keith's voice carried an aggressive tone heard all the way across the garden. "For someone who's got an awful lot of suspicion around him, I'd say you're in the wrong place."

Callum stared directly at Keith now, remaining calm. His hand curled into a fist, but he slowly tucked it into his pants pocket. "Rowan was a part of my lab team, and I'm here to pay my respects. You're the one who doesn't deserve to be here."

Anabeth and her father rushed up to both of them at the table. "Is everything all right here?" her father asked, shifting his gaze between them.

"Ask the arsonist over here." Keith squinted at Callum. "I'd be awfully curious why he's here if I were you. Did your failed experiment get out of control, or did you just mean for the whole place to go up in flames?"

Callum pointed a finger at Keith's chest. "When are you gonna stop bullying people and be a real man? I know Rowan finally realized how pathetic you are."

As Keith moved closer to Callum and drew his fist back, Anabeth's father intervened. He moved his body between the two of them and pushed Keith back a few steps. Anabeth stepped in front of Callum and gave him a disappointed look.

"You should leave," Anabeth said to him, searching his face for answers.

Autumn and Simone watched the scene unfold before them. Callum let out a sigh and dropped his head as he walked toward the entry and out of the garden. Anabeth's father shot his arm out and pointed Keith toward the exit as well. Leaving in a huff, Keith tugged at his tie and yanked it off his neck as he went out the back way.

Anabeth rubbed her fingers in circles at her temples and turned to scan the rest of the garden. The girls headed over to her, and Autumn touched her shoulder.

"Hey, Anabeth. How are you holding up?" Autumn gave her a tight-lipped smile.

Sighing, Anabeth hugged them both. "Oh, thanks for coming on such short notice. I just got really overwhelmed with all of this, and I needed some friendly faces I could trust right now."

"Yeah, that was quite a scene just now." Simone grabbed a cup of water off the table and took a sip.

"Well, Rowan sure knew how to pick 'em." Anabeth rolled her eyes and crossed her arms over her chest. She hesitated for a moment and then reluctantly asked, "Did either of you happen to catch any weird witchy vibes off those guys?"

Simone exchanged a glance with her cousin and then shifted back to Anabeth. "I mean, that Keith guy holds nothing but low energy. He's got a bloodred aura with strands of gray within it. That tells me he's angry and willing to fight, but also there's a confused dullness there. Maybe he's just lost his way."

"And the lab manager?" Anabeth's curiosity kicked in now, and she waited eagerly for Simone's next response.

"He's . . . a peculiar one." Simone shrugged. "Dark and mysterious with a very pale cornflower-blue aura. I find him to be very contemplative, even in the face of anger."

Autumn glimpsed a familiar firefighter uniform at the front of the garden. She watched as the fireman faced Rowan's photo and paused in thought.

"What about him?" Autumn nudged her cousin to direct her attention. "Up there by the photo of Rowan." Simone and Anabeth both followed Autumn's gaze to the man in uniform.

"Hmm." Simone took in a breath as she got a sense of the man's aura. "I feel a deep sense of love and loss around him." She tuned in a little closer and took a step forward. "There's an undertone of jealousy, though."

"Perhaps for something or someone he couldn't have?" Autumn watched as the man turned around to reveal his nametag and confirm her suspicions.

Fire investigator Alick Carson had showed up to get one last look at his secret love. He quickly paid his respects and then headed out a side entrance without speaking to anyone.

"That makes three suspicious men showing up this evening, two of which caused quite the scene." Autumn turned to form a close circle with Simone and Anabeth.

Simone widened her eyes over the rim of her cup as she took a swig of water. "Yeah, one guy who's a serious loudmouth, one staying cool as a cucumber, and one trying to slink away into the night."

Anabeth's gears turned as she thought out loud. "Well, if journalism has taught me anything, it's that making a lot of noise creates a good distraction, and those who keep to themselves usually do so for a reason."

Chapter 13

The sun blazed down from straight above the next day, and Autumn twisted her hair into a loose bun at her neck to cool off. She waded through the large crowd standing on a bluff overlooking the forest below. Speakers blared with announcers calling for the next round of racers to join the starting line. People in the crowd cheered as their favorite mountain biker's name got called, and Autumn felt the unhinged nature of the crowd.

"Wow, this is some event!" Eve called out beside Autumn. She had taken the day off from the Forest Brew to join the coven since Autumn had asked everyone to attend. Lainy was running a bit late after her martial arts class, but she was heading their way shortly.

"Yeah, who knew the mountain region had this many intense mountain bike fans?" Simone looked around at all the people in racing T-shirts, sneakers, and ripped jeans. "It's a rally!"

Autumn grabbed a flier from a girl handing them out in the crowd. "Let's just keep our eyes peeled and see what we can find out, okay?" She ran her hand over the flier, trying to sift through the names of all the races and see if anyone stood out. Toward the middle of the list, she spotted Keith Bryant. "He's here."

She peered up over the crowd to get a better look at the racers, when someone nudged her side.

"Hey, I made it." Lainy put her hands on her hips and looked over Autumn's shoulder at the flier. "What are we looking at?"

Autumn handed her the flier. "Keith Bryant, the racer who's also Rowan's ex-boyfriend. I'm not sure who the firefighter is in the race, though. See anyone you recognize on the list?" Lainy ran through the list as Autumn had.

"Oh, I know Mairi. She's new to the IT department at city hall." Lainy tilted her head and thought for a moment. "I'm pretty sure she used to work for the university, but I met her recently at a city hall event."

"What does she look like?" Eve questioned. "Maybe we can pick her out or they'll call her up to the starting line?"

Lainy shrugged as she stood on her toes to get a better look over a large group of people in front of her, even though her tall figure usually peered over most people. "Honestly, I have no idea how to tell anyone apart down there. You'd have to know their helmets and gear, I guess, because they're all completely covered."

Autumn moved to the side and made her way toward the very edge of the bluff. She stared down at the racers and caught the eye of someone. Judging from the bike with hand-drawn stickers all over the frame that she had seen parked at the university lab, it must be Keith Bryant.

With his helmet and goggles on, he stared right back at her, only he plainly saw who she was. They stood locked on to each other for another moment before someone nudged Keith and gave him a thumbs-up. The person followed Keith's gaze to Autumn and stopped just as he had. Autumn noted a dark-purple riding jacket and pants. From what she could make out, the racer also carried the emblem of a snake wrapped around the arm of their jacket.

Autumn's necklace warmed at her chest, and she laid her palm over it as she kept her eye on the racers. As she did, the wind picked up, and the ancestors' voices whispered on the winds.

"The forest keeps the secrets. Watch the ones who take to the trees."

As the whispers lingered on the breeze for another moment, Autumn knew the riders carried their own secrets. But with a race full of participants biking through the trees, how could she decipher who exactly the ancestors meant for her to watch?

"What do you see?" Simone snuck up next to Autumn and followed her gaze down to the riders.

"Base of the bluff, two o'clock. I'm pretty sure that's Keith and his mountain bike gang." Autumn lifted her chin in their direction just as the announcer started up again.

"And now the Peak Performance team, please take your positions at the starting line." The loudspeaker echoed across the crowd, and Autumn dragged her eyes away from Keith as he skidded away toward the start.

She glanced over the crowd as the announcers gave their last calls for the racers, and she paused at a couple large fire engines positioned on the far edge of the bluff.

"The firehouse brought their engines," Autumn said as she pointed in their direction.

"Well, why don't we go over and have a chat for a while?" Simone shrugged and took a few steps toward them. "I mean, unless we'd rather drink ourselves silly like the rest of the crowd while the racers are off shredding in the woods?"

"I'm good with going to see the firefighters," Eve chimed in. "I feel the earth pulling me in their direction, so maybe there's something to that."

"I feel it, too," Autumn agreed as she began walking. "Let's see who came out here today."

The four of them made their way through a side section of the crowd as the speaker called for the start of the race.

Everyone around them cheered loudly as a bullhorn sounded, and Autumn watched the racers trailing off into the woods between barricades and flagged ribbon.

Chief Halpin stood at the front of the fire engine with his arms crossed. He shook his head and grinned to himself as the racers all disappeared. Turning to check the crowd, he found Autumn and the girls before him.

"Autumn! Well, this makes twice in a matter of days, doesn't it now?" The chief smiled at her.

"Hello, Chief." She smiled warmly and followed him to the back of the engine. "You know Lainy, and this is my cousin Simone and my friend Eve." As she pointed them all out, they nodded at the chief.

"Nice to meet you all. Please, come back and grab some water. It's getting warm out here." Chief Halpin raised his arm to usher them toward a large orange cooler inside the back of the chief's SUV.

"Thanks, Chief." Autumn grabbed a paper cup from him. "I wondered who you'd bring out here today. You mentioned one of your own was racing, so I figured the entire crew would wanna see the race," she mentioned curiously.

"Yes, that's right! Our firefighter Tatum races with the Peak Performance team. From what I know, he's got the record for the fastest chute run. Isn't that right, Alick?" The chief waved a hand in the air and pulled over another well-built man in his early thirties, who Autumn guessed was Alick Carson, the fire investigator.

"That's right, Chief. Tatum holds the chutes record." Alick smiled and put his hands on his hips, standing firm with his legs shoulder-width apart.

"Hey, Alick," someone said from around the back of the fire engine beside them. "Didn't Tatum introduce you to that dame you've got a thing for? What's her name, Rowan?"

Autumn sensed Alick grow hot under the collar as he peered over his shoulder at the commenter to reply. "Tatum introduced us at one of their racing parties, yeah." She watched as sorrow grew over his face and he continued. "That's over now."

"Alick," Autumn said softly, trying to appear consoling in her tone. "If you're referring to Rowan Stewart, then I'm so sorry for your loss. I heard what happened in the university fire." She squinted a bit as he squirmed.

Clearing his throat, Alick nodded. "I knew she needed to get out of that lab." He shook his head and shimmied from side to side on either foot. "It wasn't good for her, you know? Being around all those people only looking out for themselves and what they wanted. I'm just sorry I couldn't convince her before—"

The bullhorn sounded again, and the announcer took to the speaker. "Here they come, folks! It's gonna be a close one!"

The crowd moved toward the edge of the bluff again, and Chief Halpin patted Autumn on the shoulder before stepping up to peruse the crowd.

"And it's Wilcox from Peak Performance for the win!" The announcer rattled off the teams as they came through the finish line tape at the end of a steep grade. "Peak's also coming in second with Bryant, folks, and Cornerstone Racing takes third! Man, Peak Performance is on fire this year, taking the top two spots."

As soon as Autumn heard the teams being called, she stepped to the edge of the bluff and peered down at the bike gang. The finished riders formed a small circle on the far end of the dirt trails. They kept their helmets on while waving to the crowd and only raised their visors to grab a few quick drinks of water.

"Woah, check out the aura around them." Simone raised her eyebrows and flipped her finger around in a circle, pointing at the group of Peak Performance racers. "A deep orange with traces of gray. Something's going on there."

The racer with the snake emblem wrapped around their sleeve stared up at the girls once again. Raising their arm and pumping it to the sky, they received echoing cheers from the crowd.

Autumn directed her attention back to the snake racer as they lifted one wheel of their bike onto the tailgate of a large pickup truck. Then, they moved to the side of the truck, gathered up a few items into a large backpack to sling over their back, and grabbed the bike again off the tailgate.

"What's that one doing in the truck?" Simone asked.

They watched as the snake racer threw another glaring look in their direction and stormed off on the far side of the woods with Keith trailing behind them.

"Not sure what that was about, but they definitely know who we are now. And if I had to guess, they're not backing down from whatever it is they're doing. In fact, it looks like they're almost daring us to stop them."

Chapter 14

E ve propped the Forest Brew front door open for the rest of the coven as she waved to her mother inside.

"Hey, Mom. We're back from the bike race, so I can help with whatever you need." Eve's smile beamed all the way across the coffee shop. She loved being a valuable part of the coven, and for the first time, she felt like she had friends who actually understood her.

"Oh, thank goodness!" Catherine Newbury exclaimed as she poured coffee for a couple patrons and headed back to the counter. "The preservation meeting starts soon, and I was beginning to think I'd have to cover it myself. Your father's gone to pick up some supplies, so I could use the help." She wiped her hands on her apron and sighed with relief. "How did the race go, girls?"

Autumn flopped down on a counter stool beside Anabeth and Finn, who had been grabbing a bite there already. "Interesting," she noted to Mrs. Newbury. Keeping her voice low, she continued so that only those at the counter could hear. "There's definitely a strange energy around those bikers."

Simone huffed behind her. "I'll say. They looked like they had more on their agenda than just winning the race."

Anabeth scanned their faces and looked at them curiously. "What do you mean? What kind of agenda?"

"The kind that plans to get into trouble," Lainy interjected as she scooted onto a stool on the other side of Finn. "That is, more trouble than they're probably in already."

"So you think they're up to something?" Anabeth questioned as she stuck a french fry into her mouth.

"No question." Simone flagged down Eve behind the counter, wrapping her apron around her waist. "Eve, what's the latest specialty? I'm starving." Simone bent over the glass pastry case and perused it.

"Oh, you're going to love my new lemon blackberry cake! It's super scrumptious!" Eve pulled open the back of the case and dragged out the tray with the cake. "Want some?"

"Oh, yeah. I'll take a slice with a chicken salad and a raspberry iced tea." Simone glanced up at Autumn. "Are you having dinner here for the preservation meeting tonight?"

"I'll grab a bite really quick before it starts. It's been a while since we've had a meeting, so I hope everyone's here. We need to review each store's plans for the Sun Day Shopping event and make sure their decorations are in keeping with the town's historic charm." Autumn sighed, already tired from the day.

The last few months had been exhausting with events, store upkeep, and running the preservation committee in place of Gran. That didn't even count her new role as the four-points witch and solving all the mysterious happenings to maintain balance in the mountain region. She had been handling it all up to this point, but something had to give. Unfortunately, her relationship with James sat on the back burner for now, even though she knew that to be the one thing she wanted more than anything.

"Right, the Sun Day event! I'm so excited for all the customers!" Mrs. Newbury chimed in. "Graham has our plan for the coffee shop, and he'll be discussing it this evening." She waved her hand through the air. "Autumn, I'll whip you up a chicken salad along with Simone's so that you can eat before the meeting. Lainy, I'll get one for you, too."

"Thanks, Mrs. Newbury." Autumn smiled. "We appreciate it."

"Hey, while you wait for your food"—Anabeth checked over her shoulder for anyone listening before she continued—"tell us the latest updates on Rowan's case."

Autumn twisted her stool to face Anabeth and Finn. "I think her ex-boyfriend Keith is our best lead right now. Although, I've gotta say that Callum at the lab and now Alick are awfully suspicious as well."

"Alick? Who's Alick?" Finn yanked a notebook and pen out of his back pants pocket and jotted down the name.

"The fire inspector, Alick Carson." Autumn said his name slowly so Finn could get the whole thing. "Anabeth, did you know he had a thing for Rowan? He wanted her to run away with him."

"The fire inspector?" Anabeth scrunched up her nose and thought for a moment. "Rowan said she met someone who treated her better than Keith did, but I didn't know who it was. I tried to encourage her to pursue that relationship, but she kept finding her way back to Keith." She shrugged and shook her head. "She always did like the bad boys."

"Well, a fire inspector could access the right supplies to start, say, a lab fire." Finn's eyebrows shot up. "Not to mention, it sounds like there's some jealousy there. That's all you really need for a situation to go wrong."

Worry enveloped Anabeth's face, and she stuffed another fry into her mouth to hold back the tears.

Autumn put a hand over Anabeth's to comfort her. "I know this is hard, but we're figuring it out. We're gonna keep an eye on Alick, but at this point, I just don't know that he's the one we're looking for."

"I'm still betting on Callum, the lab manager." Finn nodded and took a swig of his lemonade. "He's got dark alchemy written all over him, and we already know he needed grant money to maintain his research. The lab fire may have taken out the computer system, but Rowan did suspect him of accessing department files. Case in point . . ."—he opened the messenger bag beside him and pulled up a screen on his phone—"I found this." Handing the phone to Autumn, he continued while everyone gathered in to listen. "Three years ago, he got kicked out of another university for suspected tampering with experimental materials."

Simone leaned over Autumn's shoulder to read the screen. "You know as well as the rest of us, Finn, that it'd be pretty easy to tamper with everything in our state, if you know what I mean." She shot Finn a look and nodded. "I bet he tried to keep his gifts under wraps as best he could, but it just came out and someone saw something."

Autumn nodded in agreement. "Yeah, but did something similar happen again this time, only worse?" She handed the phone back to Finn. "That one might be open to interpretation, but it gives us precedent as far as his behavior, I suppose."

As they all thought about the possibility of the lab fire being caused by Callum, Eve pushed through the kitchen door with salad plates balanced on her forearms.

"Orders up! Three chicken salads." Eve put the plates down in front of the girls and walked over to the pastry case. She pulled out a piece of the lemon blackberry cake and slid it over to Simone.

A chill ran through the air as Autumn watched, focusing on the blackberries spilling over the top of the cake. "Uh, Eve?"

Something told her that cake held important properties for the evening ahead.

Eve perked up. "Yeah, what do you need, Autumn?"

"How much of that cake do you have?" Autumn peeked into the pastry case from where she sat.

Pulling out the large cake tray again, Eve sat it on the counter. "I have the whole cake! Would you like some, too?"

"That would be great. A slice for all of us, please. And actually . . ." Autumn lowered her voice again. "What kind of boost does this particular cake have?"

Pleased at someone asking, Eve sliced the cake and whispered, "Protection, strength, and connection across the veil."

Autumn turned toward Simone and exchanged a glance. "Across the veil, huh? In that case, we each need as big of a slice as we can get."

"Uh-oh." Lainy leaned forward on her stool from the far side of the counter. "I don't know if I like the sound of that. Unless the preservation committee is hosting a seance tonight, then I'm not sure I wanna know why we need to cross the veil or have an extra bit of protection."

Staring down at the cake as Eve sliced it up, Autumn twisted her lips to the side in consideration. "Don't question it. Just eat the cake." She grabbed a small cake plate from Eve and nodded. Then, one by one, Eve handed out cake plates to the others.

As they all finished their meals, members of the preservation committee slowly trickled into the Forest Brew. Mayor Halpin pushed the front door of the coffee shop open as he fervently talked to Vera Cunningham.

"Vera, you know I won't budge on the funding for this year's Sun Day. Just make it work, please." Mayor Halpin walked past everyone at the counter and waved a hand in the air. "Good evening, everyone! We're heading back for the preservation meeting. Don't mind us! Autumn, see you in a moment."

Autumn nodded and wiped her mouth with a napkin. "Yes, Mr. Mayor. I'm headed in—" Just as she glanced up, she noticed James walking in with Ben beside him. Suddenly, the stress of the last week melted off her as she watched him slide across the tile floor toward her.

"Evening, stranger." James kissed Autumn's lips softly and lingered for a moment as she pressed her hand to his cheek. "I knew this meeting would be a good excuse to see you."

Smirking as she grabbed for his hand, Autumn agreed. "I actually thought the same thing."

Simone turned to find Ben hovering behind her and did a double take over her shoulder. "Uh, hello. Were you gonna say anything or just stand over me weirdly?"

Ben laughed and rubbed a hand over his jaw. "No, I was just gonna stand here until you noticed me. I like making you squirm." He bent down until he was at eye level with her, and she had no choice but to kiss him in front of everyone.

Rolling her eyes, Simone wrapped her arms around his neck. "Happy now?"

Nodding slowly, Ben let a smile creep over his face. "Yep, I sure am. Although, I'd be even happier if you let me take you out again sometime soon. Maybe after this vote is over. I came in to distract myself from it with coffee."

"Oh my god, the vote!" Simone dropped her arms and screamed, almost deafening everyone at the counter. "Sorry, I almost forgot we've only got a few more days to cast our votes for sheriff." She shot Ben an apologetic look. "I mean, I didn't forget. It's just been busy, but I'm casting my vote tonight, promise."

"You better! If you don't want some random bloke from down the way becoming sheriff of this town, then I better be able to at least count on all of your votes." Ben put his hands on his belt as his father usually did and shook his head. "Geez, if I can't even get my girl to vote for me, I'm toast."

"Your girl?" Simone stood up from her stool now and looked him straight in the eye. "I'm your girl now?"

"No, I was talking about the lovely lady in the back corner over there." Ben chuckled as Simone jabbed him in the ribs. "Yes, you. Geez, woman. You'll be the death of me yet, I swear."

Eve rose up on her tiptoes from behind the counter as she dried a glass with a towel. "Don't worry, Ben. You have my family's vote. We wouldn't want Hollow's Glenn in anyone else's hands but yours." She looked down the line at everyone sitting at the counter. "Oh, I mean, all our hands, of course."

Autumn smiled at Eve as she chewed the last bite of her lemon blackberry cake. "I second that, Eve. Ben's got my vote as well. In fact, I already submitted mine a few days ago. Some of us aren't procrastinators." Autumn turned to glare at her cousin. "And you're right about all of us, Eve. I'd like to think Hollow's Glenn is in good hands with us."

Finn cleared his throat and got up from the counter. "I hate to break up this party, but I've got a fire inspector to check up on, and I do believe Officer Walsh's vote may be the least of his problems tonight." Finn gave Eve some money to cover the meal before he tilted his head toward Ben's silenced radio on his hip. The bright blue screen had flashed several repeated messages that had gone unnoticed.

Autumn glanced down at it and then over at James beside her, giving him a concerned look. She felt a strange pulse of fearful energy permeate through the air as she paused for a moment.

"People are in danger." Autumn stood and watched Ben to confirm.

"The Ridgeline Inn across town caught fire." Ben continued scanning the messages scrolling over his radio and then pulled out his phone just as the mayor ran out of the back room.

"Ben! What's the status?" Mayor Halpin looked concerned.

"I'm on it, Mr. Mayor. Looks like a downed tree in the road blocked two fire engines, and they won't make it anytime soon." Ben moved his eyes between Autumn and Simone. "Think I could get a little help with this one?"

Autumn nodded and kissed James. "Ask Vera to hold down the fort here for me." She gathered up her backpack and waved her hand for Lainy to follow. "Looks like that blackberry cake will come in handy after all."

Chapter 15

Black smoke plumed around the outside of the Ridgeline Inn. Autumn could barely see through the sooty air, and her lungs burned with each breath.

"Sulfur," she murmured, and searched around as Ben came rushing out of his vehicle beside her, Lainy, and Simone. "Ben, wait! Come here." She reached for him and Simone. "The air is toxic. We need a spell before we can help everyone get out of the inn."

Simone shook her hand eagerly in the air as she thought. "Sage. What about sage?"

"Yeah, that could work." Autumn nodded as she choked out a breath. "Quick, look around the edges of the property for any fringed sage growing by the trees."

The four of them spread out, squinting and hovering lower to the ground as they searched. Autumn brushed her hands through some low-lying bushes while hearing the nearby screams for help in the inn.

"Ancestors, direct my search. Lead me to that which may clear the air and reclaim these people." Autumn pressed her hand firmly to the earth and felt a vibration leading her to the left. She trailed her hand along the dirt until it reached a bush with slender leaves and a smell all too familiar.

"This is it!" Immediately, she grabbed several stalks of it by the palm and yanked them off the bush. "Thank you, ancestors and elements." Stumbling back toward Simone's SUV, Autumn called to the others. "I've got it! Over here."

Simone and Lainy appeared through the thickening smoke with eyes half-closed while Ben checked for people around the perimeter as best he could.

"Okay, what's the spell?" Simone stared at her cousin.

Autumn held the sage up in her left hand and closed her eyes. Then, she blew a deep breath into her right hand as she thought about the destructive use of fire brought to Hollow's Glenn. Anger rose within her, and from her palm, a small flame rose. She brushed it along the sage leaves to ignite them.

"Squeeze in close and focus your energy on my words." Autumn blew out softly to allow the smoke of the sage to waft through the black air. "Earth, air, fire, and water, I call upon you now. Cleanse the toxins and sweep fresh air through these trees. Snuff out the flames and leave only fresh rain in its place. With the power of three, so shall it be."

Simone and Lainy whispered together, "With the power of three, so shall it be."

Soft tingles accompanied speckled magic as it crept up the girls' hands and into their arms. The specks lifted from their skin and emerged into the air, wafting through the smoke and dissipating it around them.

Ben called from a distance, "Whatever you're doing, it's working!"

"Help us, please!" The cry came from inside the Ridgeline Inn.

"Ben!" Autumn squinted through the lightening air to find him. When she locked eyes on him, she continued. "The fire's still spreading, but the sulfur shouldn't be dangerous in the air any longer. See if you can get anyone out of the inn. We'll put out the flames so they don't spread further into the woods."

Simone ran to him and kissed his cheek. "Just yell if you need us, Chief."

With her words, Ben inhaled a fresher breath and ran toward the inn with strength. He searched the front and along the perimeter for an unobstructed open door or window, pressing on every opening he could and feeling for heat behind them.

As he came upon a side window, Ben pried a latch open enough to crack it. He paused for a moment, concerned about the potential for an explosion, but the smell of sulfur in the air had completely gone. He risked breaking the window entirely as he tore the arm of his sleeve at the seam and used it to wrap his hand. Punching a larger break into the pane, he ducked underneath it and covered his head just in case. Air howled through the opening, but the structure remained intact around it.

Ben sighed with relief as a rush of people scurried up to the window from inside, gasping for air.

"Get us out, please!" someone shouted.

"Stand back," he replied as he calmly broke out the rest of the glass and allowed the first woman to hoist herself through the window. As people made their way through the opening, Ben grabbed them on the other side.

Meanwhile, the girls heard sirens in the distance but pushed further into the woods beside the inn. A soft meow sounded at Autumn's feet, and she looked down to find her favorite tabby cat beside her.

"Tavish, how in the world did you get here?" Autumn bent down to rub his head. "Never mind, I'm glad you're here. We could use your help. Lead the way."

The cat scurried ahead, making his way through the falling branches and ashes in the forest. Autumn squinted to watch something moving through the trees ahead just as the cat stopped.

She watched as a vision of an older woman in a flowing dark-purple gown glided behind tree after tree, carefully eyeing Autumn as she moved. The woman hesitated behind the appearance of a large black iron cauldron resting on a bonfire on the forest floor. The cauldron billowed with smoke as it bubbled away with a white substance oozing from it.

"Come forth, dream walker, and walk between our worlds," the woman called to Autumn on the wind.

Autumn took a few more steps forward through a denser smoke stuck within the trees. "Who are you?"

"Autumn, where are you going? There's only a mist of rain, and we need to stop the fire from spreading." Simone looked at her cousin with concern and then shook it off to focus on the sky herself. Lifting her palms at her sides, Simone slowed her breathing. "Water within me, draw upon the sky. Allow these clouds to pour down rain and quench this earth. Put out the flames and bring calm once again."

As Simone spoke, flames rose on the trees beside her and sparks flew across the ground below. She focused her energy and raised her hands, pulling them down toward the earth as if pulling the rain along with them. With the motion, lightning sounded in the sky and heavier drops of water fell upon her head. They picked up speed quickly until the forest grew drenched with rain.

Autumn continued staring off into the distance with Tavish now by her side as the cauldron before them continued to bubble away. "Tell me who you are," Autumn repeated to the vision evading her.

"Cerridwen." The woman's voice lingered on the wind. "I walk between the worlds now blurred. For someone tries to pierce the veil without permission."

"Are you not really here?" Autumn asked, as intense sensations of light and dark bounced through her simultaneously as she spoke. She squinted as the intensifying rain pummeled the cauldron before her into disappearance, along with the vision of the woman transmuting into a raven flying away. Shaking off her trance, Autumn felt Simone shaking her.

"Cuz, I found something." Simone stared into Autumn's eyes to check her awareness.

"Yeah, okay. Show me." Autumn nodded and looked down at Tavish, who was soaked to the bone but still by her side. "Good cat."

Simone hastily moved through already muddy ground to where water pooled in a circle. "I found markings here. As far as I can tell, there's one large circle drawn in the dirt around these two trees." She crouched down and pointed. "And then there are those two stones inside the circle, each one carrying a horseshoe symbol. One right side up and one upside down."

While Autumn studied the markings, Tavish pushed against her leg, not allowing her to move within the circle. "Okay, Tav. I won't go inside it." Relieved, the cat backed down and began licking at its wet paws.

"What do you make of it, cuz?" Simone glanced at her cousin, trying to read her mind.

Autumn shook her head with disgust while tears and rain both streamed down her face. "That I'm tired of people abusing this town and the people in it. And that I'm ready to confront whatever this is because I just saw into the world this alchemist intends to cross. I felt the light and the dark they seek to entangle, and I know now that I'm the one who needs to unravel them."

Eve's Raspberry Streusel Muffins For Empowerment

For the muffins:

2 cups + 1 Tbsp flour

3/4 cup sugar

1 tsp lemon zest

1/4 teaspoon salt

2 tsp baking powder

1/4 baking soda

2 eggs, large

3/4 cup plain yogurt or sour cream

8 Tbsp butter, melted

1 tsp lemon or vanilla extract

2 cups raspberries

For the streusel:

1/2 cup flour

1/4 cup brown sugar

1/4 cup sugar

Dash of salt

4 Tbsp butter, room temperature

Preheat oven to 425 degrees Fahrenheit. Line a muffin tin with paper liners and set aside.

In a large bowl, use a wooden spoon to mix the 2 cups of flour with all the other dry muffin ingredients while chanting,

A cup of that, a cup of this. With each stir, I raise the partaker's confidence.

After stirring the mix three final times, set it aside to build its potency.

Then, in a medium bowl, whisk the two eggs. Add the rest of the wet ingredients to the eggs, stirring gently. Use a spatula to softly fold the wet ingredients into the bowl with the dry ingredients. With each sweep of your spatula, say,

Into the mix, I fold in the rest. Blend the magic together so we'll be at our best.

Add the tablespoon of flour to the raspberries and mix to combine. Fold the raspberries into the batter bowl gently.

Scoop the batter evenly into the muffin cups. Set aside and cover with a tea towel to let the magic seep in.

In a small bowl, mix the dry streusel ingredients. Cut the butter into the mixture using two forks. When the texture resembles large crumbs, sprinkle the desired amount onto the tops of each muffin.

Bake muffins for 20 minutes or until an inserted toothpick comes out clean. Place the same tea towel used to cover the mixing bowl down on the counter with a wire rack on top of it. Let the muffin pan cool completely on top of the wire rack, allowing any residual magic to rise into the muffins. When cool, enjoy!

Chapter 16

The downpour subsided, and Simone hurried out of the woods to find people stumbling around outside of what just yesterday was a historically charming Ridgeline Inn. She immediately locked eyes with Ben, who bent down over a middle-aged woman, coughing and covered with black soot.

He stood up and ran over to Simone, throwing his arms around her. "Are you all right? Are you hurt?" He ran his hands up and down her arms to check for any issues.

"No, I'm good." Simone shook her head and turned to see her cousin right behind her. "Autumn's good, too, but we lost Lainy in the chaos."

Ben nodded and looked Autumn up and down as well before a loud fire engine sounded down the road. "Okay, we'll find her. Don't worry. The fire inspector's already here, and the engine sounds like it's right behind him. But if you three hadn't been here to stop the fire, then I don't know what would've happened."

Autumn touched Ben's shoulder. "We did what we needed to do, all of us. Go on and help everyone. We'll find Lainy."

Ben agreed and gave Simone another squeeze before moving back to another man on the ground who needed help.

"Where's Tavish?" Simone looked around the scene, as the smoke had mostly cleared.

Rubbing her hand over her face, Autumn let out a little chuckle. "Not sure, but I'm not worried about that cat. I don't know how he gets all over town to help us out, but I'm glad he does. He's probably back at the cottage all snuggled up on the porch by now."

"Yeah, I wouldn't put it past him to have a secret door into the Pine to snuggle up by the hearth either." Simone put her hands on her hips and assessed the scene. "Now, where's Lainy?"

"She can't be far. I'll look on the far side of the inn if you take the back side, okay?" Autumn made her way through dozens of people looking like they'd just had the worst day of their lives.

"Sounds good. Just send me a message if you find her." Simone tapped her temple with her pointer finger, and Autumn inherently understood that Simone meant telepathically.

The fire engine pulled up on the scene, and Autumn spotted Alick Carson heading over to meet it. He appeared familiar enough with the scene that he must have been there for quite some time now. She wondered if maybe he'd been there all along.

As she rounded the corner to the other side of the inn, Autumn's locket warmed intensely at her neck. She grabbed for it and kept moving forward to see a woman with long, wavy dark hair facing the other way. The woman pulled a couple of elderly people to their feet while keeping her back turned. While she pulled a man up, the oversized collar on her shirt fell over her right shoulder, and Autumn spotted a tattoo peeking o ut.

Taking a few steps forward, Autumn squinted to see the image of a snake eating its tail on the woman's arm. She moved closer and called, "Excuse me."

The woman tilted her head slightly over her shoulder in Autumn's direction but did not reveal her features. She walked toward the trees that surrounded the inn as Autumn continued calling to her.

"Wait! Were you inside the inn?" Autumn questioned as the woman drew further into the trees at a quicker pace.

"Miss, please!" An older man on the ground beside Autumn raised a hand toward her. "I can't stand up. I think I twisted my ankle trying to get out. Can you help me, please?"

Autumn nodded and bent down beside him as she continued staring out into the trees, trying to find the woman with the snake tattoo. With no luck, she focused on the man and touched his ankle as he winced. Instantly, she knew he needed a cast and most likely some rehabilitation.

Chief Walsh rounded the corner and sighed as he spotted Autumn. "I knew I'd find you here somewhere." He walked over and bent down beside them. "Word is we have you and your crew to thank for this fire not spreading across the whole county."

Autumn shrugged. "Simone and Lainy, mostly. I just gave them a little boost, and Ben got everyone out. Except we haven't found Lainy yet." With her words, Autumn felt a few wet drops land on her skin. She looked up to see a dripping gutter from the edge of the building, and she knew Simone was calling for her.

"Chief, I think Simone may have found her." Autumn stood up and touched his shoulder. "Are you okay here?"

"All good. You go find her." The chief smiled. "My crew's got this now."

Autumn turned and sensed her cousin's energy pulling her toward the back of the building. She quickened her pace until she rounded the back corner of the inn. Yet, as soon as she did, she stopped dead in her tracks.

A river of silver liquid ran along the ground in front of her from straight out of the inn and formed a curving path toward the woods. She hurried along it until she came to the trees. Lainy stood in a pool of the silvery liquid with Simone beside her, hovering over another alchemical symbol, this one being even more intricate than the last.

Fire Chief Halpin held the door open to his office as several people, including the girls, trailed in to find a seat. He glanced out at the busy fire station full of rescue workers organizing their gear after the inn fire. They looked haggard and beat up. The chief closed his office door and nodded at Mayor Halpin to proceed.

"Well, then." The mayor started with a sigh. "This has been quite an eventful evening, and I know we're all tired. But something is going on in the region, and we need to get to the bottom of this once and for all before we lose anyone else. Ian, Ardie, what's the count from today?"

Chief Walsh stepped up and responded, "Ben's got the counts. He was the on-scene commander, so I'll let him go over everything."

Ben pulled out his phone and ran through his notes as he wiped a tired hand over his forehead. "One dead, twenty-six wounded, two critical. We got extremely lucky to even have those numbers, if I'm being honest. It could have been a lot worse if the MacKinnons hadn't been there. They did the job that we couldn't."

"We just did what needed to be done to keep everyone safe." Autumn gave him a tight-lipped smile. "But I'm glad we were there, too."

"Although, I don't know if putting out fires is really getting us anywhere productive." Simone threw her hands up in the air. "I mean, what have we actually got to go on right now? A bunch of random symbols and some silver liquid on the ground?"

"Simone's right." Lainy spoke up abruptly. "Someone is definitely taking things further, and we can't let this happen again. Chief Halpin, what do you know about this silver liquid I now have all over my legs?"

Ardie Halpin sighed and ran a hand over his chin. "Well, I'll be blunt with you. It's not good. Liquid mercury's what that is, and you need to be over with the medics to keep getting it off. So I want you there as soon as we're done. But, I wish we could let Alick in on our discussion because he knows a heck of a lot more about this stuff than I do."

"Ardie, we can't—" Mayor Halpin firmly interrupted his brother.

Holding up a hand and nodding, Fire Chief Halpin continued. "I know, I know. He's still a suspect in all this . . . Even though I know he's not involved. Still, he would tell you that mercury doesn't burn, but it can be toxic. So I honestly have no idea why it was all over the ground out there. What I do know, though, is that the same sulfur smell that permeated the air at the inn fire today drove the fire at the university lab."

"That's why we've requested a warrant to search Callum McIver's property." Chief Walsh cleared his throat and took a step back, waving Ben forward. "Sorry, force of habit. Ben, you go ahead."

Ben nodded and continued. "Right, well, the warrant went through about half an hour ago. So I suspect our officers will head over to him right about now. We already have evidence that his access card at the university allowed someone into restricted areas. If he's also got any materials on his property that we found in these fires, then we'll arrest him."

"So he's still the primary suspect, then?" Simone questioned. "But why would he start a fire at the inn? That makes no sense."

"Maybe he intended the fire for the forest around the inn, and it got out of control," Lainy suggested. "From what we've found out, he needs grant money for his forest fire research. More fires equal more of a need for research."

"That just doesn't feel right, though." Autumn stared out the window behind Chief Halpin's desk and shook her head. "I don't think it's Callum. His energy may be a little dark, but it's not malicious as far as I can tell. I don't think it's him." She sat in a daze for a moment as everyone waited for her to continue. "Chief Halpin, tell me about the sulfur. We've found salt, mercury, and sulfur now."

"Salt? Where did you find salt?" Mayor Halpin raised his eyebrows in concern.

"Someone brushed it all over Anabeth Greenwood's doorway when they tried to break into her house a few days back. We think whoever's doing this knows she was looking into Rowan's death and getting close. So they marked her door with some kind of salt substance."

"Oh, dear! Ardie, this is serious." Mayor Halpin turned to face Autumn directly. "Salt, mercury, and sulfur! We're getting into territory that I fear may be beyond most of our capabilities, unless you girls . . ."

"I know, Mr. Mayor, but we have the four elements and the ancestors on our side." Autumn pulled her gran's locket from under her T-shirt collar. "They'll be here for us again now." She said the words more to reassure herself than anyone else.

The others in the office with magical abilities sat mesmerized by the golden shimmers within the gem of the locket. Chief Walsh and Ben, the natural-borns in the room, glanced at each other for a moment, exchanging a questioning look and then shrugging.

"Autumn, the sulfur." Fire Chief Halpin cleared his throat and then refocused on the question at hand. "It's highly toxic and extremely flammable. We had to take serious precautions at the lab fire, and if you hadn't performed a spell in the air at the inn, well . . . I hate to think of it."

"But what does it have to do with alchemy?" Simone leaned forward on the edge of her chair. "And what were the symbols marked into the stones in the woods and on the ground beside Lainy? If none of us know, then we need to find someone who actually does."

"It's time for the elder." Autumn exchanged a glance with her cousin. "We have the symbols, the materials, and the three marked people." She pointed to Lainy's leg stained with mercury and gave her a sympathetic look. "Next, we need to understand how they go together and why."

"Or to just arrest the person responsible and get that out of them." Chief Walsh leaned over as Ben checked his phone.

"Callum's being hauled in now." Ben started walking toward the door. "We found a couple plastic containers full of sulfur powder hidden in the trunk of his car beside a few other items. Looks like it was enough to arrest, so we better go."

Chief Walsh nodded at his son and looked around the room at the others. "The hot springs are what we're looking for . . . out past the mountain bike trails in the woods. My first assignment was parkland security out there, and I can tell you the sulfur consumes the ground in the springs. If you go out far enough, you'll smell it."

Autumn sat up straighter at the suggestion and knew instantly that something residing in those woods carried their answers.

"Beyond the mountain bike trails," Autumn repeated while a vision of large steaming pits rose in her mind.

The chief opened the door to follow Ben out. "It's the best bet for getting sulfur around here, but . . . do I have to say it?"

Shaking her head, Autumn understood his hesitation. "No, Chief. We'll be careful and stay out of trouble."

Ben glanced through the door at Simone and chuckled under his breath. "I'll believe that when I see it."

Chapter 17

Autumn, Simone, and Lainy wearily headed out of the fire station through city hall square, where only a few lantern lights pierced the darkness. They silently made their way toward the front of the police station to find a couple people rustling around on the ground.

Lainy quickened her steps to help them gather a bunch of papers strewn around the ground in the dark. She piled several sheets and handed them to the woman beside her.

"Oh, Mairi!" Lainy smiled at her. "You're working late tonight." She turned to the other person beside her. "And Finn?"

Finn snorted. "Guilty. I'm just out doing a little research, that's all."

"Yes, and I had to grab a few things from city hall." Mairi smiled as Autumn and Simone walked up beside them as well. "I guess he and I didn't see each other out here in the dark."

Finn questioned Mairi. "Oh, you work at city hall with Lainy?" He pointed to the stack of papers appearing to be financial documents. "In the finance department?"

Mairi shoved the papers into a manilla folder she carried in her other hand. "No, I'm in IT."

Finn stared at her curiously for a moment when Autumn interjected with a realization. "Are you the Mairi who likes to mountain bike?"

Lainy put her hand on Autumn's shoulder and smiled. "Mairi, this is Autumn and Simone. They're relatives of mine, and we all went to the bike race the other day."

"Oh, relatives of Lainy?" Mairi shoved the folder under her arm to shake their hands. "Nice to meet you. Yeah, I started racing again not too long ago, but I've been riding since I was a kid."

"It's quite a sport." Simone raised an eyebrow at her. "I don't know how you do it."

"Well, it's just a side hobby that keeps me fit." Mairi took a step back from the group just as Autumn felt a pang of warmth at her chest.

She placed her hand over it to sense the warning, but a loud commotion came from outside the police station.

Mairi scurried into the dark. "I better get home for the night. See you all again sometime."

The group's attention stayed focused on a bunch of police officers around their cruiser.

Autumn craned her neck to see. "What in the world?"

Simone shrugged as they inched closer. "Who knows? The station's got all kinds of crazy things going on at all hours. Ben's phone goes off all the time with the latest."

The four of them stopped under a large maple tree that anchored the corner before the station. They watched the officers pull a man out of the vehicle and across the parking lot.

"Ah, finally!" Finn spoke up. "The reason I came out here at this hour."

"I'm telling you, this is a mistake!" The man in handcuffs yelled. He flipped his dark-black hair away from his face with a big head shake, and Autumn recognized Callum McIver through the darkness. "I just need to make a phone call and get this sorted out."

"Once we process you, then you can have your phone call," one officer said as he pulled Callum's elbow further toward the station.

While squirming through the officer's tight grip, Callum noticed the group watching him under the tree and squinted to see them better.

"Hey!" he shouted at Autumn and Simone. "You're the ones who've been looking around the lab, aren't you?"

Something told Autumn to step further into the light and hear what he had to say. She moved away from the maple and into the light of a lantern.

"Autumn, what are you doing?" Simone whispered, and tried reaching out to pull her cousin back, but she had moved too far away.

"Tell me why this is a mistake," Autumn shouted at him.

Recognizing Autumn, the officer paused for a moment and allowed Callum to respond. Callum breathed heavily as he looked at her under the light and watched the slight shimmers radiating around her aura. Judging by her features and her prominence around town, he inferred she held substantial power.

"Because I believe in the balance, and I wouldn't jeopardize it." Callum gave her a calm look that Autumn read as genuine.

The officer tugged at Callum's arm again. "Come on. Let's get you inside."

Another officer walked up to the group and nodded. "Evening, everyone." He turned his attention to Simone. "You're out late tonight. Did you come 'round to see Ben?"

Simone realized it was one of Ben's best friends on the force. "Hey, Adam. We're just coming from the fire station after being at that inn fire. It's been a long night."

"Oh, yeah." He rubbed the back of his neck. "You all right? I heard on the radio that fire was a nasty one. Ben seemed to hold it together, though."

Simone shook her head and wrapped her arm through Autumn's beside her. "We're good, thanks. Just trying to clear out the lungs with a little walk on our way home. This is Lainy and Finn, and you remember my cousin Autumn, right?"

"Of course, yeah. I see Autumn around the station every so often. It's good to see you again, and I'm glad you're okay." Adam smiled and started turning back toward the station.

"Hey, Adam?" Autumn lifted a hand to stop him. "Do you mind if I ask what made you arrest Callum?"

"Oh, so you know him?" He raised an eyebrow as Autumn nodded in confirmation. "Well, we found evidence linking him to that university fire, and it was enough. So, the rest is for the lawyers."

"So you found chemical substances at his home?" Autumn pushed a little, but as soon as she asked, she knew he was uncomfortable.

Adam cleared his throat and stared at Simone for a moment, wondering if it was a good idea to say anything more. He sighed and pulled out his phone from his pants pocket. After scrolling a bit, he placed the phone down on the ground.

"Seems I lost my phone just a minute ago in the rush to get the perp inside." He threw his hands up in the air. "Sure would be nice if someone found it for me and brought it back into the station." Adam gave Simone a wink and took a few steps back, leaving his phone on the ground in front of them. "Anyway, nice to see you, Simone. Sorry I couldn't say anything more about the investigation, but stop by the station anytime."

They all stared down at the phone in surprise. As soon as he was a few steps away, Autumn snatched it up and looked at the screen.

"He's got evidence pictures." Autumn ran her finger over the screen to move through more images. "Looks like they're from Callum's car." Standing under the lantern light, she squeezed in closer to the others so they could all see. "It looks like containers of sulfur in the trunk and some papers on the floor of the back seat."

"Is there a closeup of the papers?" Simone wondered what would have been on the documents to verify Callum's guilt.

Autumn stopped to read a photo of a document. "That one's an angry letter to the university grant board. Sounds like he wasn't happy about getting passed over for a grant."

"I mean, that could've sent him off the deep end. Keep scrolling." Simone lifted her chin to suggest Autumn move on.

"Oh, what's this?" Autumn paused at an image of Callum's laptop. Over a screensaver image of him and a friend, it showed a file folder labeled "Ridgeline." As Autumn continued swiping, the girls looked at images that showed emails and calendar screenshots from university officials.

"What is all of this?" Simone looked at her cousin, unsure of how these screenshots mattered.

Finn analyzed the image as Autumn zoomed in. "Judging from the photo, the police found these screenshots on Callum's computer. Looks like a bunch of schedules from university staff."

"Yeah, and they're all showing a meetup at the Ridgeline Inn tonight." Autumn sighed and lowered the phone.

Lainy's mouth widened at the realization. "The fire. He knew they'd be there."

"Wow, that's a strong case for an arrest." Simone paced around a bit in the shadows of the lantern light.

Autumn stared off toward the police station. "It appears that way, yeah. But I don't know. Something tells me we're not seeing what really happened."

"You don't think he did it? Even with all this evidence?" Simone grabbed the phone from Autumn and started sifting through the photos herself.

"I've never gotten an eerie feeling about Callum. Dark, yes, but eerie, no. I just don't feel it. Do you?" Autumn eyed her cousin to get a sense of what she felt as well.

Simone shook her head and twisted her lips to the side as she thought. "No, I don't. But if not Callum, then who? The ex-boyfriend?"

"My money was totally on Callum before." Finn pointed to the fire station at the back of the square. "But we happy few, we band of brothers." He poked his finger into the air continuously.

The girls stared at Finn blankly as he gave them an exasperated sigh. "It's Shakespeare, geez. Don't any of you read? Firefighters loyally stick together, and I bet they won't talk when it comes to the fire inspector. I'm leaning toward it being him."

Autumn thought for a moment. "He was at the Ridgeline awfully fast tonight when everyone else got stopped by a tree in the road. Still, I'm not convinced that they're the band of brothers we should look at." She started walking the phone back to the police station, when a beeping noise sounded on the far side of the station.

"What's all that about?" Simone questioned as she peered around the back corner of the building.

A vision popped into Autumn's head. "Callum's car!" She ran toward the building and stood against the back corner to watch as a tow truck pulled Callum's car into an underground parking lot with signs marked "Police impound lot. No trespassing."

"That's the car from the photos?" Simone eyed it, trying to match the details from what she'd seen.

"Yep, that's it. They must be keeping it for evidence." Autumn moved forward a few paces as the tow truck pulled in further. "Do you see that? On the wheel well, there's something smeared in yellow."

The tow truck disappeared with Callum's car into the underground garage before anyone else could get a look.

"Hold on," Finn said, grabbing Adam's phone from Autumn and pulling up the photos again. "Maybe we could see it in one of these images."

Autumn looked over Finn's shoulder as he scrolled. "That one!" She pointed to the screen as he paused on an image.

Autumn zoomed in on the wheel well to see the symbol of a triangle drawn over a cross.

"Looks like someone drew it with a stick. Probably with the yellow sulfur the police found in the trunk." Finn handed the phone back to Autumn.

"But Callum wouldn't draw that on his car, would he?" Simone questioned.

"Highly unlikely," Finn responded.

Autumn shook her head and tapped the phone in her palm. "No, he didn't. Someone marked him just like the others. So now we have all three primes, just as Mayor Halpin said."

"Salt, mercury, and sulfur." Lainy sighed deeply. "Of course, I had to go and step in the mercury."

Finn gave Lainy a curious look and opened his mouth to say something, but Autumn put her hand on his arm.

"At the inn fire tonight." Autumn swallowed hard.

Lainy shook off her emotion and refocused. "We have all the basic ingredients. Plus, the solstice is fast approaching for an added boost of fire energy . . ."

"Then, all the alchemist needs now is time to organize their final formula and . . ."—Finn exchanged a serious look with Autumn—"complete the process to activate the spell."

Chapter 18

The next morning Anabeth pushed through the front door at Parchment and Pine with a large to-go tray of drinks in one hand. Tavish watched her curiously from his perch in the shop window amongst all the celestial garlands and summer solstice decorations.

"I'm here with coffee, tea, and scones for everyone." Anabeth strode to the back counter where Autumn and Simone stood waiting for her. "What did you need me here so early for, anyway?"

Lainy pushed through the front door next, dragging her sunglasses off her eyes with a tired look. "Let's get the show on the road. It'll help me wake up before I need to be at city hall."

Simone jumped up from behind the computer with more energy than she usually had first thing in the morning. "On it. I'll get the book."

"What book? And what show?" Anabeth eyed them all curiously.

Autumn put the invitations down that she was sorting and came around the counter. She put her hands on Anabeth's shoulders and sighed. "Anabeth, you're in the loop now about our magic, so we're going to use it as best we can to protect you."

Lainy peeked into the bag of scones that Anabeth had left on the counter and grabbed a raspberry streusel one, stuffing a piece into her mouth. "We're both marked, so we need to up our game."

Sighing, Anabeth pulled her shoulder bag off and dropped it to the floor beside a counter stool. "Lainy, could you speak in plain English, please? What do you mean we're marked?"

Exchanging a look with Lainy, Autumn waved Anabeth back to the hearth room. "Whoever is behind the fire at the university and at the inn last night also marked you and Lainy. We think they're working on some type of alchemical process, and it's possible you're part of it."

Anabeth stopped at the archway to the hearth room and glanced at the three girls. "All right, now you're scaring me.

My cousin just died, and you think the person who did it also marked me for something? And Lainy, too?"

"Oh, and the guy who's the prime suspect in the lab fire. Callum?" Lainy choked down another piece of a scone as she nodded.

Autumn tilted her head at Lainy and gave her a look. "Okay, I know it sounds crazy, but yes. That's the gist of it."

Simone pulled out the MacKinnon family Book of Spells on the circular table that sat before the fireplace. "Relax, Anabeth. We've got a spell for everything. You'll be fine."

Throwing her hands up in the air, Anabeth nodded and rolled her eyes. "Great, yeah. A spell for everything, and you've even got an ancient spell book right there." She plopped down in one of the wingback chairs beside the hearth and took in the scene before her. "How did I never catch on to this whole witchy underworld before?"

Autumn drew the hearth room curtains closed and smiled at her cousin. "Thanks for grabbing the book. I wish we could've done this later at the cottage, but we couldn't wait. Besides, today's gonna be a long day. We've gotta gear up for the Sun Day event."

"Hey, how did you get that obscure key to appear so you could get the Book of Spells, anyway?" Lainy popped the last of her scone into her mouth and brushed off her hands like she was ready. "I thought it needed to be a dire circumstance to open your gran's wardrobe?"

"Not dire, no." Autumn hesitated as she thought. "The ancestors just need to sense the right intentions for what lies inside." She shrugged as Tavish trotted in, nosing his way underneath the heavy curtains. "Thankfully, they must've known we really needed some help after the inn fire last night."

"Works for me. So, which spell are we using?" Lainy peered over the book as Simone flipped open the pages on the table.

"Maybe it's best that the book decides for us." Autumn stood beside Simone and nodded for her to stop flipping.

Simone lifted her palms in surrender and took a step back. "You got it. We'll let the book do its thing."

Autumn lifted her palms up to her sides and spoke aloud. "Elements and ancestors, hear our call. Guide us to a purifying spell to rid the marked energy and keep it at bay."

A strong wind flew down the fireplace and into the hearth room, sending the scent of cedarwood along with it. Autumn turned toward Simone, as they both felt their gran in the room.

The book's pages flapped against each other furiously, going back and forth to find the requested page. Once it stopped, the book revealed a double-paged spread before them.

Autumn leaned in and ran her finger down the page to read aloud. "Purifying spell to subdue hexes, curses, and the like."

Simone peered over her shoulder. "Ginger and milk thistle. Right, let me just pull those out of my back pocket really quick."

Chuckling under her breath, Autumn shook her head. "I'll text Eve. She's waiting for my call since I knew we'd need some extra ingredients. If she doesn't have it, then she'll run by Aunt Jo's shop and grab them there. Between Eve, Jo, and my mom, they're bound to have it all."

Autumn pulled her phone out of her back pocket and started messaging. Meanwhile, Tavish scratched at the fireplace behind her. "All right, Tav. We have a few minutes to start the fire for you."

"I'll grab the other ingredients." Lainy stood up from a wingback chair and looked over the book. "White salt, black salt, sage, and a white candle carved with a Celtic shield knot. I'll do my best."

Lainy pulled the draped curtains back and walked out into the shop to peruse the offerings. "Candles are in the hutch drawers, right?"

"Yep!" Simone called to her. "And the salts and sage are in the mason jars beside Aunt Penny's tea bags."

Anabeth watched as they all busied themselves around the shop, looking for spell ingredients. "I feel helpless. What can I do?"

Autumn threw a few starter logs onto the fire and gave Anabeth a pursed smile. "Anabeth, you're not helpless. You should know that by now."

"Got the goods!" Lainy walked back into the hearth room with an armload of ingredients.

"Here." Autumn grabbed two white taper candles and a small knife with a wooden handle from Lainy. She handed them to Anabeth beside her. "You're going to make the protection symbol on the candle."

"Like those sigils that Rowan had all over her apartment?" Anabeth took the items and waited for Autumn to respond.

"Well, not quite like those symbols. We don't think those were exactly sigils, after all." Autumn tried to put it in terms Anabeth would understand. "However, we draw our symbols to be an unbroken chain of intention."

"Oh, okay." Anabeth moved toward the table, giving Autumn a confused look. "But how do I make the symbol?"

Smiling, Autumn turned to grab a long, skinny stick from a pot near the fire. She pulled a few ashes forward from the bottom of the fireplace as the rest of the fire sparked behind it. "Let me show you." She moved the stick through the ashes, drawing as she spoke. "Celtic knots carry the energy of our ancestors and the land, sea, and sky. When we create them, they serve as amulets for protection and strength of our people. The shield knot holds great power for protection."

Nodding along, Anabeth watched the drawing appear in the ashes. "Okay, so this shield knot will protect against the markings?"

"That's right. The symbol looks like a pie divided into four slices. When you draw each slice, you start by drawing a heart. As you reach the end of the heart at the top, you keep it going down into the center of the shape, weaving it into a circle and then back out. Then, you ensure that each slice you draw connects to the next, like this." Autumn finished connecting the shield knot on the bottom of the fireplace and looked up at Anabeth to be sure she understood.

"I think I've got it." Anabeth took the knife and began forming the symbol on one of the white candles, just as Autumn had instructed.

"There's really no wrong way to do it, as long as you have the right intention." Autumn patted Anabeth's shoulder. "You're infusing your energy into the candle. Just remember that our intention lies in purification and protection."

"I'm purifying and protecting. Right." Anabeth continued carving the blade into the candle with a bit of nervousness. "My first spell, and it had to be for protection. Why couldn't it have been for financial abundance or something more fun?"

Autumn laughed just as Eve peeked through one side of the curtains. "There you are!" She moved around the side of the table to help Eve come into the hearth room.

"I come bearing gifts!" Eve smiled widely, but then realized her smile may be inappropriate and flattened it quickly. "I mean, not that this is an occasion for celebrating. Sorry, I didn't mean to imply—"

"It's okay, Eve." Anabeth finished up the candle and placed it down on the table before grabbing the second one. "As long as you keep making those astoundingly good pastries of yours, then I won't ever be mad at you for anything."

"I'll second that!" Simone popped through the curtains to join the rest of them, and Eve regained her smile at the comment.

"Do we have enough time for the spell now? What time does the shop open?" Lainy questioned.

Autumn waved a hand through the air. "We're good. The shop doesn't open for another hour. Besides, I have a feeling our first customers won't be in for a while, and it'll be a late night. How about the rest of you?"

"I cleared my calendar this morning," Lainy chimed in. "After the fire last night, my boss wanted me to take the day off, but I told him I'd be in later."

Eve shrugged. "My mom's good with me being here this morning since I already prepped the pastries for the day. Anyway, she never minds when it's coven business."

"And I'm good, too," Anabeth said with a slight upset in her voice. "The paper's got me reporting on the downtown renovations now since they took me off the fire investigation. Finn asked for my help with research and all, but it's not my story." She threw her hands up. "So my time is your time!"

The four coven sisters looked at Anabeth with regret. They all knew Rowan's death had shaken her, and now the perpetrator targeted her as well. She put on a brave face for them, but each of them felt the anxious energy around her.

Autumn sighed and wrapped her arm around Anabeth for a bit of comfort. "Well, looks like we don't have any excuses. So as Lainy suggested, we'll get the show on the road."

Chapter 19

Tavish brushed against Autumn's leg as she picked up the Book of Spells. The cat meowed and shook its tail with delight, knowing magic would soon carry through the air. Autumn laughed at the cat as she moved to the opposite side of the table in the hearth room.

"You're right, Tav. It's time for a spell." Autumn placed the book down on the table once again and pulled together a few of the materials that Simone had brought into the room. "Lainy and Anabeth, squeeze together in front of the fireplace. First, we'll blend our spell materials together."

Eve pulled open a small jute bag she'd brought from the Forest Brew, with several small mason jars. "Here's the ginger and milk thistle."

"Perfect. Here we go." Autumn ran her finger down the spell book again. "Elements of earth, air, fire, and water, we call upon you now. Bring together your energies to purify these two souls before me. Rid the harm that marks them. Shield them from the dark."

Autumn looked through the materials on the table and pushed a few of them toward Eve. "With white salt, ginger, and milk thistle, we detoxify the marks."

Eve used a small wooden spoon to get a heaping tablespoon of each ingredient and place them into a heavy granite mortar bowl. "Detoxify," she repeated as she poured the ingredients together.

"With black salt, we shield from dark intentions." Autumn pushed the black salt jar in Simone's direction.

Repeating the process, Simone scooped a tablespoon of the black salt into the mortar and grabbed the pestle to crush all the ingredients together. "Shield," Simone said aloud as she pummeled the bits together into a sand-like texture.

Autumn nodded to her cousin, and Simone snatched the bowl up, placing it in the crook of her left arm. With her right hand, she drew pinches of the salt mixture up and spread them across the floor. She moved in a clockwise direction, starting behind Lainy and Anabeth at the fireplace and going around the table.

Sprinkling the last of the mixture on the floor, Simone placed the bowl back on the table. "The protection circle surrounds them."

"Okay, Lainy, you do the honors." Lifting the two white candles Anabeth had carved, Autumn handed them across the table.

Lainy grabbed them and turned to the now-roaring fireplace behind her. Careful not to move beyond the salt line of the circle, she ensured the candles lit sufficiently and placed them back in holders on the table. "With our ancestors' energy, we shield."

Then, Lainy took the bunch of sage wrapped in brown twine from the table and held it over the flame of the first candle and then the second. As the sage bundle sparked with a gentle flame, the girls watched tiny shimmers lift from the tip into the air.

Pulling the sage closer between her and Anabeth, Lainy blew out the flame. Then, she wafted the light plume of smoke over the center of the table for a moment.

Autumn lifted her right palm as if leading an orchestra. "Sage to clear residual energies and ward off unwanted ones."

With Autumn's words, Lainy swirled the sage in a clockwise motion around her head and Anabeth's and then down around both of their bodies. She continued as Autumn repeated the words.

"Clear and ward. Clear and ward. Clear and ward." Autumn watched as the smoke plume glistened with hints of golden shimmers and lingered around the two girls. "May their energies stay true and together be anew."

Lainy turned to face Anabeth with the sage stick. She lifted Anabeth's right hand to the sage so that they both held it together.

"As we say it, so shall it be." Autumn nodded, and the others all followed her in repeating the final words once again. "There's one final step to seal the spell." Autumn lifted one of the white candles in her right hand and extended her left. "Lainy, your wrist, please."

"The wax?" Lainy gave Autumn a questioning eye.

Autumn nodded, and Lainy understood what the spell called for. She graciously lifted her right palm to the sky and offered Autumn her wrist. Autumn took it in her hand and used her other to tilt the burning candle over Lainy's wrist. Hot wax dripped from the flame and onto Lainy's skin.

Wincing at the heat, Lainy pulled her arm back slightly. Autumn let two more drips fall onto Lainy's skin before letting go. "With fire, we seal the spell."

Next, Autumn reached for Anabeth, who hesitantly offered her own wrist. Autumn repeated the process, and Anabeth bit her lip as the hot wax dripped onto her. She sighed with relief as Autumn finished and the wax cooled against her skin.

"Thank you, elements and ancestors, for your support. We close this circle now, and may the elemental balance always be within us and without." Autumn closed the Book of Spells and turned toward Eve. "Would you mind grabbing the besom

I have in the back office? If we collect the spell materials, I bet my mom would feed her garden with the remnants tonight."

Eve smiled and nodded. "Good idea! I'll grab it." She scurried out of the hearth room right away.

Tavish stretched his long legs on the floor beside Autumn before wandering over to the fireplace and jumping onto the base.

"Well, I guess someone got his cozy spot back." Autumn smiled, looking into the dancing flames of the fire.

The deep hues of the flames drew Autumn in, and her eyes clouded over for a moment. A vision of a crone standing in the woods flashed before her. Smoke billowed around the woman, who held up a spell book and then dropped it down into the flames at her feet. Autumn felt a sudden urgency to retrieve the flaming book and lunged toward it.

"Autumn!" Simone yelled, stirring Autumn abruptly from the vision.

Lainy and Anabeth grabbed Autumn's arms tightly and pulled her back from the edge of the fire.

"The book . . ." Autumn looked behind her for the MacKinnon Book of Spells, which still sat on the circular table, just as she'd left it.

"The spell book?" Simone narrowed her eyes at her cousin and then at the family heirloom. "You just lunged at the fireplace. Are you okay?"

Eve trailed in, smiling and holding up the besom. "Got the broom!" She looked around the room at everyone's confused faces. "Uh, what's wrong? Did the spell not take or something?"

Simone closed her eyes and shook her head. "No, Eve. It's fine." She came around the table to grab Autumn's elbow and bring her even further away from the fire. "Just a little mishap, that's all."

Eve accepted the response, and Lainy and Anabeth helped her gather up all the materials to clean the room while Simone looked over Autumn.

"You had another vision, didn't you?" Simone leaned back to assess her cousin's aura. "You've got dark-purple streaks in your aura. That's not like you."

"I saw the crone from the inn . . . Cerridwen. She told me I was walking between worlds." Autumn swallowed hard and met eyes with Simone. "I think she's also the woman from James's dream, and I don't know why she keeps appearing to me."

"Autumn, you didn't tell me her name was Cerridwen." Simone sighed. She turned to pull open the curtains to the hearth room and let more light into the space. "This is—"

"Hello, dears!" Penny's voice called from the front door. She glanced back to the hearth room as hints of smoky shimmers made their way beyond the archway and into the center of the shop. "Oh, is there a spell in the works? Should I come back?"

Autumn shook her head and walked toward the front. "No, Mom, it's great timing, actually. Eve's bottling up the spell remnants for you to take back to the garden. We did a purifying spell on Lainy and Anabeth. Turns out, the alchemist marked them both for something.”

Penny gasped and covered her mouth with her hand. “Oh, dear! What did you use for the purifying spell? Did you include milk thistle?”

Autumn placed a hand on her mother’s arm to calm her. “Yes, Mom. We got the recipe from the Book of Spells, and it’s all taken care of.”

“Except . . . for those visions and what the markings actually mean.” Simone crossed her arms and gave Autumn a look. “Go ahead. Tell her.”

“It’s nothing, really.” Autumn gave her cousin a glare. “I’ve just been seeing that crone in more visions lately.” She pulled her hair back from her shoulders and twisted it together at one side.

“That crone.” Simone rolled her eyes. “As if it’s not a big deal that she called herself Cerridwen.”

“Cerridwen,” Penny repeated under her breath. “Earth below, that is quite the goddess to call in!”

“A goddess?” Autumn eyed her mother. “Who is she?”

“Oh goodness, I fear we’ve fallen short in teaching you the stories of old. She’s the ruler of death, transformation, and rebirth, my dear.” Penny went to the wall hutch where her teas sat and sorted through them as she spoke. “A symbol of the three phases of maiden, mother, and crone. It makes sense considering what you told us of your previous vision. Stories say she shapeshifts through many forms. She's been a crone each time you've seen her?"

Autumn nodded. "Yes, a crone, but I also watched her transform into a raven at the inn."

"Knowledge and death." Penny held up a few kraft paper bags of teas to read the labels. She stopped as she came to one labeled "Beyond the Veil" and handed it to Autumn.

"Mugwort and blackberry tea." Autumn thought for a moment. "That's why we needed the lemon blackberry cake the other night before I saw her."

Penny sighed. "She called to your thoughts. Be careful, dear. In the hands of a dream walker, these ingredients carry potent energy. But Cerridwen is cunning, and you must be as well if you're dealing in her world."

The others gathered around them now at the hutch and eyed the tea pouch in Autumn's hands.

Eve leaned in and eyed the ingredients. "But what does piercing the veil have to do with alchemy?"

"You said the girls bore markings?" Penny tilted her head with curiosity. "Tell me what you've found."

"We found salt, mercury, and sulfur at the incident sites of the two fires and Anabeth's home after the break-in attempt," Simone chimed in. "So we know the alchemist has the prime components they need, and it's only a matter of time before they complete some kind of spell."

Penny shook her head. "Not a spell, an energetic process. You see, alchemy exists more as an ancient science of energy transmutation. Elemental magic goes beyond just transmutation alone, but even alchemical workings in the wrong hands, well . . . let's just say we don't want to find out what happens, especially if the practitioner also bears magical gifts."

"Dr. Carmichael mentioned only going to see the elder about this when we were ready. I didn't see any patterns with all of this before, but now . . ." Autumn stared at the tea within her hands, focusing on the words "Beyond the Veil." She tapped her finger on the bag and looked at her mother. "Now we know there's a process at work here, and it appears to be tapping into something beyond our world."

"I'll set up the introduction, and Jo will go with you." Penny gave her daughter a tight squeeze. "And I think perhaps he'll be just as interested to meet you as you are to meet him."

Chapter 20

Jo rounded the rocky corner on a one-lane mountain road in Penny's borrowed Range Rover. She leaned over the steering wheel to peer up at the trees jutting out from the cliff beside them.

"I wish Penny would have driven us out here today, but we've made due. Almost there." Jo smiled and clenched her hands tighter over the steering wheel, doing her best to stay calm around the bends.

"I should have driven, Aunt Jo. You didn't have to." Autumn gave her aunt a look that saw right through her stubbornness.

"Nonsense, I have to feel out the directions. It's not on any map, you know, so it's best I drive." She spun the wheel around a hairpin turn and made Autumn swallow hard with nervousness. "Besides, this gets me out of my comfort zone, which doesn't happen often for someone my age." She stopped the car under a line of aspen trees with bark as white as the winter snow. "Ah, we're here!"

"Um . . . we're on the side of the road, Jo." Autumn released her seat belt hesitantly.

"Precisely. It's a bit of a hike from here. We just can't go any further by car." Jo pushed the car door open and took a deep breath of mountain air. "Oh, it's wonderful up here!" She brushed off her brown riding pants and stepped out, crunching the dirt beneath her tall boots.

"If you say so." Autumn got out of the car and put her backpack in the trunk, taking on a few essentials in her pockets.

As they took a few steps, the aspens shook around them in the wind. A beautiful rustling sound echoed through the tree line, and Autumn felt the deeply rooted earth energy of this place.

"This way, my dear." Jo stepped carefully toward a drop-off right beside the car. She grabbed on to a sturdy tree branch and eased down a dirt path. As she disappeared from sight, Autumn scurried to find her.

"Aunt Jo?" Autumn stopped at the edge of the drop-off and looked down to find Aunt Jo a few feet down. "Oh, okay. I guess I'll follow." Grabbing the same tree, Autumn mimicked

Jo's footsteps and carried herself down the path toward the bottom.

"Now then, we'll be on our way." Jo smiled and continued forward on a single-track path through archways of scrub oak trees and undergrowth. She pushed through hanging branches and lifted them high for Autumn to squeeze under as well.

They came to a small spot on the path where the trees opened up and a whole panorama unfolded before their eyes. Autumn took in the gorgeous rolling hills of the mountain region covered in a brilliant green.

"What a view! I've never been on this side of the mountain before." Autumn shook her head in amazement.

"Few have, dear. This constitutes protected ancestral land, and you need permission from the elders to be here." Jo patted Autumn's arm. "But when this elder found out you were coming, access was without question, of course." Jo began walking again as Autumn thought about her words.

"What do you mean the access was without question? I don't understand." Autumn leaned in closer to her aunt, who stopped abruptly right in front of her.

"Autumn, my dear, you are the four-points witch now. This is your dominion as the energy keeper of the earth, air, fire, and water of the mountain region. The energy that flows within these lands also flows within you, as you are one. No one else can lay claim to these lands because you are bound to them. Just as all other elemental witches are bound by our covenant to protect it. And by it, I also mean you."

"So you're saying that I rule over these lands?" Autumn squinted through the trees to look beyond them into the mountains.

"Not rule the lands, exactly. You are the lands. And the sea and sky, which you know." Jo turned her head over her shoulder for Autumn to really hear her while she walked. "You hold the energy within you, so no one can discern where these lands end and you begin, child."

Autumn put her arm out to touch a tall aspen tree standing beside the trail. She felt the tingles of its energy course through her hand as if giving her a welcoming hello. She smiled and pressed her palm firmly on it while sending a gentle warmth back as a thank-you.

A cool breeze swept through all the surrounding trees and rustled the leaves once again. A couple trees in front of them turned their branches inward over the dirt path and created an archway.

"My goodness, you are very welcome here." Jo smiled and nodded. "Thank you, trees."

"Yes, thank you, trees." Autumn continued under the archway, taking in as many details of the path as she could.

She heard the tapping of tiny critters along the bark of the trees, wings flapping in the overhead tree canopy, and even the stretching of blanketing moss over nearby logs. With each sensorial step, she became more receptive to the idea of claiming this mountain forest as her dominion.

"We're here," Jo said with a sigh. She pointed ahead to where the trees opened up before them.

Autumn glimpsed a mounded, cave-like structure set into the mountain with grass and moss covering the outside, and she recalled a similar vision she'd had. "It looks like a house out of a fairy tale."

"Yes, I suppose it does, doesn't it?" Jo nodded and moved into the clearing.

As Autumn followed, mushrooms lifted straight out of the ground beneath their feet and shimmered with golden magic. They lined a path for them directly to the front door of the inset cottage.

"He knows we're here. Come." Jo marched through the mushrooms toward the rounded wooden door surrounded by mossy stones, several of which carried interesting symbols. Jo reached out to grab the iron door knocker, but the door creaked open on its own.

The aromas of honey and smoked cedarwood wafted from inside and grabbed their noses, pulling them inside like a magnet.

"Shut the door behind you," a voice called from deeper within the home.

"Of course, Arailt." Jo waved Autumn inside and closed the door behind them. The sound echoed through the cozy cottage and sent a vibration through the air.

A tiny, bent-over man with whitish-gray hair walked out from a back corner carrying jars of tinctures in his arms.

"Don't mind the vibrations. They just keep me informed of the house happenings."

He propped his armful of jars onto a raw edge wood desk and brushed off his hands. Then, he wrapped his hand around the stalks of a potted plant and twisted to yank a bunch out by the roots. He brought it over and grabbed Jo's hand, leaving the bunch in her palm.

"A borrower never forgets, Josephine." He shook a finger at her. "Those cuttings will bring many blessings to your moon garden, just as you once brought to my wife."

Jo's face warmed as she remembered the woman he spoke of. "I was quite fond of Labhra, and I was sorry to hear of her passing."

Arailt stared off into the distance for a moment, recalling his late wife as well. As he came back to the moment, he shook off the memory and lifted his right palm through the air. A pop came from the back of the room, and Jo and Autumn turned to find an iron cauldron hanging inside a stone fireplace that had just been lit.

Coming over to Autumn, Arailt grabbed her hand. "Let me have a look at you." He ran his finger over her palm and made curious noises under his breath as he examined it. "And what have you come to ask me?"

Autumn glanced over at Jo, who gave her an approving nod. "Well, sir, we think there's someone dabbling in ancient alchemy in Hollow's Glenn. There've been two fires, and a few have now died. We're trying to figure out who's doing this and why."

"And you think I have the answers to this?" He busied himself near the fire as they spoke.

Looking around him, Autumn noted stone runes stacked in a large basket on a wooden stool. The large wooden mantle behind him held ancient carvings, and baskets of viny plants hung from the ceiling over his head.

"I think you can help us understand the ancient wisdom," Autumn said matter-of-factly.

"Because I am an ancient?" Arailt laughed under his breath. "What do I know?"

"You know of the prime materials that we've found. Salt, mercury, and sulfur. You know of their attributes and how to change them. And I'm guessing you know what's beyond the veil and why someone would want to pierce it." Autumn's heartbeat quickened as she waited for his response. She felt the ancestral magic radiating from him and the wiseness of an owl waiting to be released from his mind.

"I may know of these things. But then again . . . you do as well." He moved closer, craning his neck to look into Autumn's hazel eyes. He watched as purple glimmers shone within them. "Ah yes, you do, fairy witch. Tell me."

Autumn exchanged a look with Aunt Jo. She swallowed hard and closed her eyes, remembering her experiences of the past year. "I've bent water and formed it with the air. I sparked the flame inside of me and brought it into true existence. And

I carried myself and others on the wind. And I've spoken through the mind with what lay in my heart."

Arailt nodded and gave her a tight-lipped smile. "And what of within?"

She opened her eyes, considering what he meant. She knew instantly as she stared down into his brown eyes he wanted to know of her inner journey. The path that had led her to this point.

"I was once a calm breeze blowing over the land, awaiting another day of the same. As of late, I'm an electric hurricane, although I currently sit within the eye. The wind, rain, and lightning I possess have tumbled me in the storm already, and I fear I may move out of the calm once again if I do not regain the connections I once knew."

"Mmmm." He moved to the cauldron and grabbed a large wooden spoon to stir the contents within it. "No one can settle the raging hurricane but itself . . . once it finds stable ground. You will do the same."

Arailt grabbed a few sprigs of herbs from a nearby shelf and crushed them in his hand before throwing them into the cauldron. He stirred the pot some more and left the spoon in the cauldron. As he waved his hand in a circle, the spoon stirred the pot itself. Then, he beckoned Jo to come over beside it.

"Keep an eye on that spoon. It has a mind of its own." He wagged his finger at Jo, and she smiled obligingly.

"You, my great hurricane, come with me." He walked to a shelf filled with dusty old books. Mumbling to himself as he perused the spines, he tapped his finger on his chin. When he came to a tall evergreen-colored book with a tattered cover, he pulled it from the shelf and walked it over to the desk under the front window.

He flipped the book open with a thud and whispered the word *Anian*, an ancient word for nature.

With one last page turn, the worn book popped completely open and remained there. Arailt leaned closely over it, squinting to see it properly. He patted the open page with his palm.

"Look here and tell me what you recognize." Arailt left Autumn alone with the book as he checked on Jo at the fireplace. He listened carefully for Autumn's response as he walked away.

Autumn eyed the page full of alchemical symbols and calligraphed labels below them. She nodded to herself as she tried to identify which ones looked familiar. "The salt symbol marked the home of my friend Anabeth. The quicksilver that Lainy stepped through carried the mercury sign, and this one." She ran her finger over a triangle with a cross below it. The symbol glowed under her touch and radiated a golden hue across the entire page. "Sulfur. The putrid scent of it remained in the air from the university fire that started this, and I saw this on the car impounded by the police."

"So you have the primes, indeed, and the putrefaction process completed in the initial fire." Arailt stirred the cauldron and patted Jo on the arm to continue. "What else, fair hurricane?" He walked back toward Autumn at the desk.

"Have you seen a circle with a pentacle or hexagram within it? What other markings have you seen? Think carefully."

"I saw . . ." Autumn turned to stare into the flames of the fire beneath the bubbling cauldron.

"Yes, child, go on," Arailt prodded her. "Let it out."

"After I saw her, I found a circle drawn on the muddy ground, and stones carved with . . ." Autumn lost herself in the flames of the fire as the face of the crone came back to her.

"The book, child! Show me the carvings." He pushed the book toward her on the desk, and Autumn gathered herself to look through it again.

"The stones held these two symbols on either side of the circle." She pointed to a horseshoe right side up and one upside down.

Arailt's face grew serious. "And who was it you saw before the circle?"

Autumn swallowed hard and stared at the elder before her but did not speak.

"The maiden, the mother, or the crone?" He rose on his tiptoes and craned his neck to look into Autumn's eyes once again. "Pig, greyhound, or raven?"

"The crone," Autumn whispered under her breath, sensing the shadowy energy of Cerridwen as she said the words, "becoming the raven."

"Well, now." Arailt turned to Jo and nodded. "We have the intention, and you have little time to waste." He headed to some tall shelves built into the back wall of the cottage and rummaged through more glass jars filled with herbs and tinctures. Grabbing a small vial of liquid, he placed it in Autumn's hand. "You'll need this."

"Okay, but what exactly is the intention?" Autumn stared at the vial in her hand. "What's this alchemist trying to do?"

Arailt huffed and scurried over to the fireplace again. This time he poured a ladle-full of the liquid within the cauldron into a tiny ceramic cup. "Drink this, hurricane." He raised it for Autumn. "You've seen the goddess Cerridwen, and you've crossed the worlds."

"Yes," Aunt Jo confirmed. "Autumn appears to hold the key to many worlds, not dreams alone like other dream walkers."

"It will be a strength to you that Cerridwen remains on your side. She has guided you in her appearances." Arailt nodded and sat on a small wooden stool shaped just for him. "The crone and the raven denote the processes nearing a close and the line between life and death being blurred—the horseshoe of life and the inverted of death." He motioned for Autumn to continue drinking the concoction.

Autumn took another sip and scrunched her face with disgust. "It's quite potent."

He chuckled as he rubbed his aching knees. "An elder cares not for the taste of things, only the result. This drink clarifies the worlds, and with it, you will know what you must do to separate them once again. For the one you seek aims to blur them, and you must protect the balance of life and death. Cerridwen only presents herself when a transformation activates, and this one appears to be very dark, indeed."

"How much time do we have to stop it?" Jo clung her hands together, pushing her rings from side to side with her fingers.

"I'm afraid time dwindles. From what I gather, the alchemist nears their final stage of coagulation. They will attempt to solidify matter and spirit, and in doing so, their formula will be complete." Arailt stood and walked once again to the ancient book resting on the desk. He turned to one of the last pages and held it up for them to see the symbol encompassing the page.

Autumn eyed the detailed circle inscribed with a pentagram and smaller circles at each of its points. Within the pentagram sat several other alchemical symbols.

"Look for a marking such as this. When the alchemist reveals a similar transmutation circle, you know the final stage has begun." Arailt moved toward the cottage door and began pulling it open.

"And this vial? When do I use this?" Autumn held up the little vial he'd passed to her earlier.

"Oh yes!" He nodded. "I'm an old man, and my mind forgets me." He took the vial from her and held it up to the light streaming into the cottage. "Chlorine from the evaporation of ancient salt lakes. A few drops should stop the formula from taking effect." He handed the vial back to Autumn and eyed her one last time. "Before you go, I have a stone circle just outside that could use a good talking-to. Would you mind? I'll just be a moment with Josephine."

Autumn exchanged a look with her aunt, who nodded at her in approval, and Autumn proceeded to the door. "I'll be outside when you're ready, Aunt Jo."

Arailt closed the door abruptly behind Autumn, and she could hear the two of them chattering away on the other side. She sighed and looked over the grounds before her. On her right, a tiny stone path made its way through overgrown grass. The stones shimmered with brilliant silver specks, and the wind picked up around her with the whispers of her ancestors.

"You're here." Autumn breathed in deeply, hoping desperately to connect with the ancestors through their normal words rather than receive strange visions.

A powerful gust blew through, calling to her. "Walk through the worlds. Become the bridge you're meant to be."

She knew they hinted at accepting her visions, but the thought of the visions continuing made her anxious. Autumn watched the tall grass blow in the breeze as the stepping stones under her feet shimmered with silver. She eyed the stones and followed them beside a stone wall covered in green vines. Her steps drew her to a wider clearing in the trees where stones twice her size stood straight out of the earth in a circle. Moving closer to one of them, she placed her hand on the edge of the stone.

Immediately, Autumn felt a pulsing energy as intense as a pounding heartbeat competing for her own. She pulled her hand back and heard the ancestral voices once again.

"Walk through the worlds. Become the bridge you're meant to be."

They prodded her to step inside the stone circle, and she hesitantly took a couple steps forward. The trees swayed furiously around it, and the wind howled. Golden streaks flew between the stones, enveloping Autumn in a spinning circle of light.

The energy intensified within her, and she felt herself leave the ground and hover a few feet above. A vision of her father, Laith, shone in her mind, along with a gathering of elders behind him. He called to her, "*Roghnaithe*," the chosen one.

Her weightless body rose further into the air, and she watched as the stones stood a few feet below her now. A line of birds flew down from the surrounding trees and swept themselves into the golden current still spinning around her. They squawked and flapped their wings in tandem with the wind as Autumn felt them bow to her.

The vision of Laith and the elders reappeared, and one of them moved forward to encompass Autumn's vision.

"Do not be afraid of the worlds within which you walk. For one day, you will not only bridge them but unite them. The ancient fae and the witches summon you as the chosen. You are our *Roghnaithe*. But you must unite the worlds within yourself before uniting those without. Start with the task at hand and know that all worlds lie within the self."

As the elder's voice faded along with the vision, Autumn's body slowly lowered back to the ground. The winds slowed, and she sat on the overgrown grass in the stone circle with soft eyes.

"Oh, that wind!" Jo called in the distance. "My goodness, the trees must have something to say! Autumn, are you ready, dear?"

Autumn stood and made her way onto the stone path once again. She peered over her shoulder at the stone circle as she walked, glimpsing a few silver shimmers settling back into the stones.

Arailt watched her intently as she came back to the cottage. "Conversations with the stones stay with you alone. They can be a rowdy bunch, but they mean what they say." He turned and gathered a flannel-wrapped bundle sitting on a long carved wooden bench beside the stone garden wall. "Don't forget this, Josephine. And thank you for doing me this favor."

"Thank you, Arailt. For everything. Oh, and I forgot to mention that Rosemary also said hello. She'll send good energy your way." Jo bent to kiss his cheek and clasped his hands in hers.

He sat down on the wooden bench, and a familiar mark caught Autumn's eye. Several overlapping medium-sized circles stained the top of the wood in the same place. It was as if something wet had sat there several times over, and her mind recalled the sweat stain of the juice cup Callum carried with him daily.

"Arailt, do you have visitors often?" Autumn eyed him curiously.

"An old man requires no visitors. Only the company of the mossy stones and swaying trees. If there were an occasion, I'd prefer it done to the point and made in haste. No time for chatty banter when there're calcinations and fermentations to perform." He pushed his palm shakily upon the bench to raise himself up. "I make only one exception to this rule, but now I have two." He gathered Autumn's hand in his and patted it in his own wrinkled palms. "My lands are your lands, fairy witch . . . Or shall I call you a fair hurricane? Either way, come when you like."

Chapter 21

L ainy pushed the door open to Parchment and Pine to find a packed shop. Her eyes widened along with a smile as she made her way to the back counter. Autumn and Simone busied themselves with customers as they boxed up celestial bunting, large paper sunflowers, and tissue paper suncatchers.

Dropping her martial arts bag on one of the counter stools, Lainy sifted out a hair tie and bunched her long, straight hair into a high ponytail. She watched the girls thank their customers as she pulled a few bobby pins from her tote, held them in her teeth, and continued to smooth her hair back before using the pins.

"The Pine appears to be the happening place today!" Lainy noted as she leaned over the counter and saw a hint of golden shimmers coming off the calligraphy pen Autumn used to write a note. "What's that?"

Autumn glanced up at her just as Vera Cunningham walked up to the register. Smiling, Autumn turned to Mrs. Cunningham and handed her a small box with the note she had just written, inserted underneath a twine bow.

"Thank you for leading the preservation meeting the other night, Mrs. Cunningham. This is for you." Autumn watched her run a hand over the box with surprise.

"For me? Autumn, you know I'm happy to take the lead on any management needs. There's certainly no need for gifts, but . . ." Vera pulled the note out and unfolded it as the girls watched her eyes dance with delight. She opened the box and pulled out two tickets.

"Thank you! Wait 'til I tell Bill that we have tickets to the dinner theater! We've been working so hard to get the restaurant ready for Sun Day that there's been no time for each other." She sighed and shook her head. "Honestly, Autumn, you never have to do anything, but thank you."

"You're welcome, Vera." Autumn waved to her as she walked toward the door.

"Uh . . ." Simone swiveled around on her stool behind the computer and gave Autumn a look. "Weren't those tickets supposed to be for you and James?"

Autumn twisted her lips to the side and nodded. "Yeah, they were, but I told you. I need to take some time to myself right now. Besides, Vera helped me out, and she runs on appreciation. So gifts go a long way with her."

"Well, I like gifts, and I run on appreciation." Lainy shrugged as the girls gave her a look. "What? I'm just saying." She lowered her voice. "Coven management should keep in mind what motivates us." She pulled a pair of hiking boots out of her tote bag and switched out her heels from work. "I'm ready to go whenever you are, Autumn."

"Okay, sounds good. My mom should be here in a second to watch the shop while we're all gone." Autumn tidied a few things behind the counter.

"Where are you headed, Sim?" Lainy looked at Simone curiously.

"Well, since my guy's the new town sheriff, I figured I'd help him move into his office." Simone lifted her eyebrows a few times and gave them a smirk.

"That's right! Ben won the election!" Lainy leaned over the counter toward Simone and tilted her head. "Did you do anything interesting to celebrate?"

"Everything I do is interesting . . . But it's no one else's business but my own." Simone got up and raised an eyebrow at Lainy. "It did include a new black jumpsuit that I looked particularly good in, though." She headed into the back office and waved a hand over her head. "I'll tell Ben you said congrats."

Lainy slapped her hand down on the counter. "Would it kill her to be more extroverted?"

Autumn smiled at the question, knowing Simone valued her privacy. She stacked a few invoices into a pile on the counter and gathered up her backpack. "Did you come from your class?"

"Yeah, I went to the earlier class tonight since you wanted me to go with you. I'm getting pretty good with my form, but I haven't done any sparring yet."

"You'll get there." Autumn paused to receive a download. She picked up a sticky note and sifted through her container of pens before lifting out the right one. After scribbling a message on the note as tiny magical shimmers lifted from the paper, she handed it over to Lainy.

"Inner strength comes when you least expect it." Lainy read the note aloud. "Thank you, I guess?"

Laughing, Autumn cleaned up the pens and paper. "Keep it in mind and maybe it'll spark something for you at the right time. Anyway, I've been meaning to ask. How's the planning for Chief Walsh's retirement party going?"

"Good, actually! Now that we know Ben will replace him, I can get the final details worked out. Then, I'll be over here ordering invitations, so you better set aside a few nice designs." Lainy wagged her finger at Autumn.

"Already got that covered." Autumn smiled and came around the counter to join her. "Ready."

"Oh, I thought you needed to wait for your mom to show up." Lainy tilted her head at Autumn in confusion.

"She's headed out of the flower shop next door now. She should be here—"

The bell at the front door chimed as Penny pushed it open.

"Now." Autumn nodded as Lainy raised an eyebrow at her.

"You're good, Autumn MacKinnon. You're good." Lainy smiled and lifted her tote bag onto her shoulder. "Okay, let's go."

Penny waved at the girls as she carried a tall kraft-paper-wrapped bouquet of sunflowers to the back counter. "Hello, girls! I'm all set to run the shop. Just thought I'd bring a little brightness in here as we get ready for the longest day." She poked around in a few cabinets underneath the counter.

"Back wall, far left corner, Mom." Autumn waved. "Tell Simone I'll see her tonight at the cottage. Thanks for watching the shop."

Penny followed Autumn's directions and pulled out a large bell-shaped glass vase. She held it up to the light, pleased with the find. "Oh, this will do nicely!" As she peered around the vase at the girls, she fluttered a few fingers in the air. "Bye, girls! The shop's in good hands!"

When they were outside on the curb, Lainy gave Autumn a sideways look. "You didn't tell your mom where we're headed, did you?"

Autumn made her way over to Lainy's new all-wheel drive Mini Cooper. "It didn't come up."

Lainy unlocked the car and threw her tote bag into the trunk. "Oh, it didn't come up, huh?"

They got into the car and rolled down the windows. Lainy pulled up a GPS map on her phone and propped it up on the dashboard. "You honestly didn't say anything? I thought you'd want a backup to the backup plan just in case of, you know, whatever."

Autumn looked to Main Street in front of them as Lainy started driving. She wondered if she should have taken more precautions than she had. "I didn't want her and Jo worrying for no reason. Besides, Eve and Simone know we're headed out to find the hot springs that Chief Walsh mentioned, and Simone's with Ben. So help is just a call away." She pulled a small Forest Brew bag from her backpack and removed a couple cookies from it, handing one to Lainy. "Eve made us these lemon icebox cookies for a little boost of fire energy."

Lainy snatched the cookie right away. "Oh yes, please!"

"Plus, I've got Gran's necklace. It'll give us a warning if something's wrong." Autumn placed a hand over her chest and felt the necklace under her cotton shirt. "There's definitely something out there that we're meant to find. I just don't know what yet."

Lainy glanced over at Autumn for a moment. "You're not usually wrong, so my money's on you. Although, I am leaning heavily toward this Keith guy being the alchemist. He's got the vibes for it, and I mean, come on. The sulfur springs sit out past the mountain bike trails he rides. Not to mention he's got alchemical drawings all over his bike, and he wanted money from Rowan. Yeah, he totally did it."

Autumn laughed. "All right, fire witch. Let's keep an open mind and not jump to conclusions. We have to find actual proof and make sure we get the right person."

"You saw him and his bike gang out there at the race. They were arrogant, biking around like they owned the place. Then, they stormed right back off into the woods after they won and didn't even bother with the podium." Lainy drove through narrow wooded roads on the outskirts of town as they crept through the cliffs into a lower valley.

"That was strange, how some of them just went back into the woods after the race . . . as if they weren't really there for the race. Maybe it was a cover of some sort." Autumn stared out the window at the rocky cliff wall wrapping around the road next to them. "Anabeth said something about a grow operation they had. I wonder what kind of land they'd need for that."

Lainy slapped her hand on the steering wheel with a thought. "Hey, you know, I should ask Mairi Wilcox. She'll probably give me the scoop on these guys since she rode with them."

Autumn stared at Lainy for a moment as they wound around another curve in the road. "Her last name is Wilcox? As in, the Wilcox who won the race?"

Nodding, Lainy tightened her grip on the wheel. "Yeah, that's right. Mairi won the race, so she must be pretty good after just getting back into racing. I think she recently joined up with that team, though."

Autumn stared out the window and thought about everyone's connection to this bike gang. Keith raced with them regularly. A guy on the team from the fire station introduced Alick to Rowan at one of their bonfire parties. Callum apparently knew them all from the lab. And now, Mairi had joined the team. Was this the band of brothers where the trouble lay?

The car turned around another bend with trees growing into the road from the cliffside. As an oncoming car passed a bit too close on the left, Lainy shook her head and followed it with her gaze, but Autumn's attention drew to the middle of the road in front of them.

"Look out!" Autumn pointed at the road, and Lainy slammed on the brakes.

Their seat belts tugged at their chests and pulled them back tightly. Lainy pushed the hazard lights on in the car and looked out the window to see a beautiful red fox standing calmly in the road. It looked back at her with dark-amber eyes.

Autumn moved her gaze from the fox over to Lainy and watched as the two of them captured each other's energy. The fox flattened its ears and lowered its snout for a moment before turning around and heading back toward the tree line.

Lainy cleared her throat and turned the hazard lights off, moving the car once again. She took a deep breath and caught Autumn staring at her. "Sorry, are you okay?"

"I'm fine. But . . . that fox spoke to you, didn't it?" Autumn adjusted in her seat and waited for Lainy to answer.

"I . . . felt its energy. We shared the same heartbeat for a moment. And then, he beckoned me to follow him further into the woods." She curved the car around another bend, and the trees opened toward the rocky dirt trails they were looking for. "I guess it's a good thing we're here, then."

Chapter 22

A twig cracked under the weight of Autumn's hiking boot, and she raised her head to see a flock of birds scattering from the tree canopy overhead. She sensed the movement echoing through the forest and making all energies there aware of their presence.

"Great, now the whole world knows we're out here." Autumn sighed. "Well, I'm pretty sure we're on the same trail the bike gang followed the race." She looked around her at the tall, spindly trees thickening further out from the path. "Something's gotta be out here." She peered through the trees ahead and felt an unfamiliar energy. "Or someone."

Lainy stopped suddenly in front of Autumn, giving her a glare. "Did you just jinx us? Or did you actually have an insight?"

Autumn shrugged. "I don't know, exactly. There's something unfamiliar out here, but I can't put my finger on it. And to be honest, I feel extremely in tune with the entire vibrating energy of the forest, so it's not like I can really pinpoint one thing right now. My senses have been firing on all four cylinders, and my understanding of it hasn't really caught up yet. I think it's the fae side of me kicking in."

Nodding, Lainy continued following the single-track path through the trees. "I see it affecting you more these days. I mean, I've only known you as the four-points witch, but I can assume it's like all the elements awakening within you."

Autumn chuffed under her breath as she watched each step of her path. "Honestly, it hasn't been that long since the other elements opened up to me. I mean, Gran's only been gone for what? Less than a year?" She ran her fingers through her long auburn hair. "This year has been exhausting, to say the least. And uncovering all these new powers and using fire and water in ways I never have before, well, that scared me, to be perfectly honest."

"And now that you know you're also fae?" Lainy listened over her shoulder while she continued through a rock garden full of various-sized perfectly round stones.

"It's different now. You know, with elemental magic, we harness the elements and become them or even transmute them. But this fae energy heightened my awareness for all energy around me and within me. It's like seeing the world in hypercolor. And the visions and dream walking . . ." She let out a breath as she stumbled down a few stones behind Lainy. "Well, that continues to push beyond my understanding of time and space."

Autumn felt a buzz in her leggings pocket and stopped to pull out her phone. "Finn's texting me. The police just released Callum. Someone paid his bail."

Lainy turned to say something, but her eye caught the hint of brilliant green light under Autumn's T-shirt. "Autumn, your locket is glowing."

Autumn stopped immediately and grabbed for the necklace at her chest. She pulled it from under her collar, and it instantly radiated heat into her palm. "I got so focused on our conversation and the pulsing energy of the trees that I didn't notice." The locket burned against her touch, and she let it go to hang gently over her shirt. "Well, it's letting me know now, I guess."

The girls looked around at the dense ground cover more prevalent where they stood now than on previous parts of the trail. Autumn stepped off the trail and bent down to the underbrush before her. She ran her fingers over a few thin strands of leaves in an aloe plant shape. Pulling a leaf off the stem, she brushed it gently under her nose.

Autumn raised her eyebrow at Lainy. "It seems we've found the grow operation Anabeth mentioned."

Lainy realized the entire forest floor sat covered in cannabis plants. "So they are growing for money." She scanned the surrounding area, making sure they were the only ones there. "We better get out of here before someone comes."

"Yeah, you're right." Autumn stood up and glanced around her for any other signs of what might be going on out there. She took another step and stumbled on a large branch but caught herself on the tree behind her.

"Are you all right?" Lainy reached out a hand to help Autumn stand up. When she put her hand on the tree behind Autumn, her hand felt the uneven texture of something underneath it. "Autumn, this tree . . ."

Autumn brushed herself off a bit and faced the tree behind her. Her mouth dropped open as she found a symbol burned into the trunk of the tree. "It's an eye." She placed her palm over the symbol to feel its energy. "Someone meant it for protection."

Lainy walked a few paces through the plants and pointed to another tree. "Here's another."

"An upside-down triangle with a line through it at the bottom. That's the symbol for earth." Autumn moved her eyes from one tree to the other. "They're trying to protect the land here for growing."

"To protect their investment is more like it." Lainy crossed her arms and shook her head. "Wow, they've got acres of untouched land out here with no one around."

"They're attempting to pay back their debts and scale the business. They have plans." Autumn moved closer to the trail and let the energy of the forest carry her in the right direction.

A wind swept through the tree canopy overhead and brought a few leaves falling through the branches in front of her. She felt the pull of a now-familiar crone's presence ahead. It drew her through the trees as they opened to a rockier terrain.

Cerridwen's face flashed in Autumn's mind as she spoke in a low tone. "The markings guide you."

With each step forward onto a rockier path, Autumn felt the heat of Gran's locket at her chest. "We better be on our toes. Keep an eye out."

Lainy nodded and followed Autumn further out. "Was it the ancestors?"

Autumn squeezed her lips together and gave Lainy a concerned look. "Cerridwen. We're getting close." She pointed to another marking on a large flat stone stacked on top of others on the ground. "I recognize that one." The marking of a triangle atop a cross appeared to be chiseled into the travertine rock. "It represents sulfur, which marked Callum's car after the inn fire."

"You mean, like the highly flammable sulfur that caused the fires to begin with?" Lainy looked all around them at the towering trees stretching into the distance. "It's not like we're standing in a massive kindling pile or anything."

"Just remember"—Autumn reached for her phone in her leggings pocket. She quickly texted Simone their location, along with a picture of the symbol on the stone—"you're a fire witch, Lainy. Fire is your ally, not your enemy. Wield it, don't fear it."

"Right, wield it. Don't fear it." Lainy jumped across a few stones as Autumn led them into a larger rocky area with a distinct sound of gurgling water in the distance. "I'm pretty sure I taught you that."

Autumn smiled and put her hands on her hips. "Yeah, actually. I think you did." She chuckled at her long-lost cousin. "I guess the student has become the teacher."

"Oh, thanks. Yeah, rub it in that you've got all these magical tricks up your sleeve now, and . . ." Lainy trailed off as Autumn raised a finger in the air.

"Can you smell it?" Autumn quickened her pace over the rocks, hopping over several at a time now. "The sulfur. Cerridwen's pulling me this way." She tilted her head around a few trees as she went and glimpsed a vision of a woman in purple dancing up ahead. Autumn continued faster, trying to catch up to the image of the crone before her.

Lainy threw her hands up. "Yeah, this is great. Let's go further into the belly of the beast," she said sarcastically. "Of course I wanna look death in the eyes today and see if I can put out the flames of a massive sulfur fire. Why not?"

The girls stopped at the edge of over a dozen turquoise-blue pools before them. Steam vented from the surface of a couple of them in the distance, and Autumn felt the water gurgling between the travertine rocks next to them. She darted her eyes around the pools, searching for Cerridwen once again, but the vision of her seemed to be gone.

"This is incredible! I had no idea something so beautiful was out here in the woods." Lainy shook her head in amazement at the pools.

"Beautiful and powerful." Autumn thought of Cerridwen just as much as the pools before her. She bent down to the hot spring in front of her. "So much heat lies under the surface here." She carefully pressed her hand to a stone, feeling the intense warmth and drawing it back quickly. "I sense all the elements converging into one at this point. There is no beginning or end to them."

"And there's no end to this godawful smell!" Lainy held a hand to her nose. "If it wasn't so beautiful, I don't know how anyone could stand to be out here."

"I guess sulfur classifies as a hot commodity to an alchemist." Autumn stood and walked around the perimeter of the hot springs. "And if you're planning an alchemical process that requires it, then what better a find than hot springs full of it?"

"So how do we stop them from taking this?" Lainy questioned.

"We can't. They've already got it." Autumn followed a few more symbols further along the stones. "But now that we know what they have, we can intervene with the process."

With her words, the sulfur smell intensified in the air, burning their throats. A strange hissing sound carried over the pools as the girls took slow steps to move away from the hot springs.

"What's that noise?" Lainy choked out.

They both backed away to the edge of the pools and stopped short of a massive rock pit of snakes rising toward them. The snakes hissed with distaste at the sulfur smell. Autumn stammered backward a few steps as several snakes coiled up onto themselves to reach higher out of the pit and closer to them.

"Those are rattlesnakes, Autumn!" Lainy yelled.

"Yeah, I got that." Autumn slowly moved her feet away, but a rattlesnake lifted and showed her its fangs with a hiss. "Yep, I definitely got that."

She locked eyes with the snake as it swirled its head slowly from side to side. Autumn felt a fearful determination in its eyes, and she knew it didn't want to fight her unless absolutely necessary.

"Hold on," Lainy moved further to the side of the snake pit and rubbed her hands together. She lifted her palms at her sides and whispered under her breath. "Heat within these lands, raise a fire on these grounds. As I move my gaze, set the rim ablaze."

Lainy moved her eyes along the perimeter of the snake pit as her hands glided in the same direction across the air. Flames sparked wildly from beneath the ground and sent the rattlesnake bending backward to fall onto the other snakes. They hissed and stirred furiously as the flames rose higher around the rim of the pit.

Using her strength and will to carefully control the fire, Lainy calculated each movement to ensure the fire stayed just around the snakes where she wanted it.

Autumn breathed a sigh of relief and stumbled back over a few stones. "Okay." Her chest heaved as she calmed her body. "Thanks. That was, uh . . . a little terrifying, but also validating."

Lainy squinted at Autumn, trying to make sense of her words. "Don't tell me you're speaking to snakes now." She slowly dropped her hands to her sides, reducing the flames even more.

Wiping the sweat from her forehead, Autumn shook her head. "No, yes . . . I mean, no. I didn't speak to the snake, exactly, but I felt its fear viscerally for a moment." She looked over at Lainy again. "Thanks for the fire, though. Good thinking. And your wielding of those flames . . . Pretty powerful."

Lainy smiled to herself as she watched the flames soften and the snakes coil up again into the center of the pit. Just as the girls settled their nerves, a crack sounded in the distant trees. Autumn jerked up to follow it with her senses. Her necklace blazed with intensity at her neck, and she winced at the heat of it.

"We're not alone." Autumn swallowed hard as a spark flared in the trees and burst toward one of the hot spring pools with an explosive blow.

A massive smoke plume billowed up into the sky with toxic fumes floating behind it. Before either of them had time to respond, a secondary explosion followed the first, and they both fell back onto the rocky ground, unconscious.

Mrs. Newbury's Shareable Cornbread Muffins For Friendship

1 cup yellow cornmeal

1 cup flour

1/3 cup sugar

1/2 tsp baking soda

1/4 tsp salt

2 eggs

1/3 cup honey

1 cup buttermilk, or 1 Tbsp vinegar plus milk to make a cup

8 Tbsp butter, softened

Preheat the oven to 375 degrees Fahrenheit. Line a muffin pan with paper liners and set aside.

In a large bowl, combine dry ingredients. Make a well in the center of the mix and add the eggs, whisking them gently while saying,

Like the comfort of good friends, with each stir of my spoon, the warmth extends.

Add the rest of the wet ingredients into the center well. Then, mix everything to combine fully and say,

Bring kinship with each bite to make everything right.

Scoop the batter evenly into the muffin pan. Tap the pan gently on the counter three times to settle the batter and allow the magic to seep in. As you put the pan into the oven, say,

Now, bake it all in and let the good connections begin.

Bake for 15 minutes. Let cool completely before enjoying.

Chapter 23

Autumn's eyes flitted open for a moment to see someone in front of her. She felt their arms pulling at her shoulders and dragging her along the ground. A wet cloth covered her mouth, and she sensed a dense air through it. As she came to, she lay under a scrub oak tree on rocky ground. Blinking through the burning sensation that stung her eyes, she opened them completely to find Callum staring back at her.

She jolted herself more awake and pushed backward against the trunk of the tree. "Callum!"

He threw his hands up quickly to show he meant no harm. "It's okay." He choked out a cough and grabbed at his throat. "I'm not going to hurt you."

"Autumn! It's all right. He pulled us away from the fire," Lainy yelled before covering her own mouth with some kind of wet cloth.

"You what?" Autumn stared at Callum, confused.

Lainy scooted closer to Autumn on the ground and checked a gash on her ankle. The bleeding appeared to have stopped. "Okay, good. You can walk." She motioned to Callum to help her lift Autumn to stand. "I could only suppress the flames so much. Their fury grew too intense, and the fumes were too strong. We need water to tame the fire, and then we've gotta get out of here. It's lucky Callum had some water and rags on hand to help us breathe."

Autumn let go of Callum and Lainy's support. She focused on the smoldering mass of fire and smoke now looming over the entire hot spring area before her. She blew out a forceful breath, and the winds shifted, carrying much of the fumes away from them. Next, she hobbled forward and focused on the hot springs themselves.

"May hot water become cool. Lift and soothe the flames above. Ease the heat, rest the fury." She rubbed her fingers together and lifted them higher into the air as water droplets from the pools lifted as well. The drops encapsulated a portion of the flames and quenched them into nothing.

Callum watched Autumn in amazement as she worked with the elements. "You're not just an air witch as I thought."

"Come on. That's enough to clear a path. It's time to go." Lainy grabbed Autumn's elbow and pulled her toward the rocky path into the tree line.

"I called for help! They'll be here soon," Callum yelled as they hurried into the trees and away from the remaining fire burning over the springs.

"Simone," Autumn said under her breath.

Lainy glanced over to her and nodded. "Can you send her a message?"

Autumn scurried through the rocks and onto the dirt path through the cannabis field. "She already knows. I can feel her getting closer, and she's bringing help as well."

Sighing with relief, Lainy turned back and gave Callum a tight-lipped smile. "Let's just get out of this forest so we can breathe again."

They fumbled through the branchy path, pushing falling trees out of their way as they went. Black smoke rose through the trees behind them, and Lainy sensed the flames still fuming on the hot pools where they'd left them.

As they slowed to catch their breath near the entrance to the trail, Autumn heard fire engines in the distance.

"They're almost here." She peered over her shoulder at the two of them. "Just a few more feet and we'll be at the end of the trail." Seeing a massive red truck through the trees ahead, she panted her way to the trailhead.

Firefighters donned in full gear rushed up to them, dragging them back to the truck. An ambulance backed up behind the fire engine, and paramedics rushed toward them with oxygen masks.

Autumn met eyes with Lainy, and they both knew Callum owed them some answers. She inhaled a few breaths of oxygen and then headed over to where Callum sat on the ground as Lainy followed.

Staring down at him, Autumn tapped into her intuition. He hadn't started that fire or put them in danger.

She sat beside him and pulled her mask aside. "Callum, I'm Autumn and this is Lainy." She gave him a pleasant look to ease his tense demeanor.

"You're the witches who think I started the lab fire and killed Rowan." Callum took another hit off the oxygen mask and then removed it. "I didn't do any of this," he said calmly, looking at the ground as he spoke. "But I think I know who did."

Lainy and Autumn exchanged glances. Autumn leaned in toward Callum. "If you know something, we need to know, too. Who do you think is behind this?"

Callum huffed. "That obnoxious biker, Keith Bryant. He's framing me at the lab." Callum raised his arm in the general direction of the university. "Trying to make it look like I've been letting someone use our computer system. I know he took my access card." He shook his head. "He just uses everyone to get whatever he wants, including Rowan." He raised his knees and sank his head lower between them. "I know she didn't like me, but I liked her. She was kind when no one else was in that lab. Until Keith made her suspicious of me."

"Rowan knew you were using magic in the lab, though." Autumn eyed him curiously, trying to put the pieces together.

"Yeah, she knew." He nodded and lifted his head at her. "She saw my drawings, and I think she heard me doing a spell one day. Not on my experiments. I would never. It was just to get other people to stop bothering me. They all think I'm strange."

"But you are an alchemist?" Lainy questioned outright.

He squinted, unsure of how that related. "Yeah, I'm an alchemist. My grandfather raised me, and he's quite a reclusive alchemist himself. He wants me to not only understand my earth magic but ancient workings of the natural world as well. So I still tend to practice away from everything else. I suppose that's why I've always been an outlier." He laughed and rested his head in his hands. "Alchemist earth witch raised in the woods by a recluse. Yeah, I never fit in."

"It's Arailt, isn't it?" Autumn smiled at Callum. "Your grandfather."

Callum gave her a curious look and turned to Lainy to question Autumn's words with her as well. "You know my grandfather?"

Autumn chuckled into her oxygen mask and removed it to speak again. "I just met him, actually, and he's quite the character. It makes sense now, though. You must be the exception to his no-visitors rule."

"I guess I am, yes. Although, I don't go by as often as I'd like, but I made it to see him recently." Callum took another hit of oxygen and rolled his sleeves up, feeling more comfortable n ow.

Autumn remembered the circular sweat stain she had seen on the wooden bench outside Arailt's cottage. "I'm sorry I thought you did all this."

"No, I'm the one who needs to apologize. I'm sorry I yelled at you the other night at the police station. I thought you were like everyone else, suspecting me for just being a little strange." He sighed. "It's never been easy for me."

Lainy played with a few stones on the ground as she considered his words. "Then who posted your bail? I mean, if everyone suspected you."

"My grandfather did." Callum shrugged. "Of course, I'm sure someone did him a favor and brought the money into the station. He never leaves the woods, but he's a well-respected man in the elemental community. So someone helped."

Immediately recalling the goodbye at Arailt's cottage, Autumn knew Aunt Josephine had done the favor. Arailt had given her a bundle of something to take with her that day. Even though she'd never mentioned the specifics of the favor, Autumn knew Jo would do anything without hesitation for a dear friend.

"Callum." Autumn looked at him, bewildered. "What made you come out here today?"

He sighed and watched the rescue workers running into the woods and radioing for helicopter assistance. "I needed to clear my head after being arrested. Usually I come out here to gather samples for my research when I need some peace and quiet. Although, I'm sure you saw the grow operation in the woods. Since they've started up, there's been no peace out here, and Keith's ragged on me more than ever. He saw me watching them and threatened me to keep it quiet."

"It's gotta be Keith," Lainy interjected. "He's got access and motive, and we've seen him with those alchemical drawings on his bike."

Callum huffed under his breath at the thought. "Alchemical drawings? Keith wouldn't know what to do with alchemy if it slapped him in the face. I've seen him in the lab, and his work barely passes snuff. There's no way he's an alchemist. A wannabe sigil artist, at best, with all that junk he slaps on his mountain bike. But an alchemist? No way."

"So he's just a poser, then, trying to make it look like he's some kind of alchemist. But if not Keith, then who?" Lainy turned to scour the faces of the firefighters. "The fire investigator?"

Autumn shook her head. "It doesn't feel like he did it." Autumn paused, hoping to receive a download, but nothing came to her.

Chief Walsh suddenly pulled up to the scene with Ben and Simone in his police SUV. Simone ran out of the car and over to the girls.

"Oh, thank god! You're okay!" Simone knelt on the ground and checked over Autumn and Lainy for confirmation. Her eyes moved to Callum, and her face turned serious. "Callum." She cleared her throat. "I'm glad you got these two out and called for help. I heard you on the emergency radio. So I just wanna say . . . thanks."

Autumn's eyes widened, and she exchanged a look with Lainy. "Well, that was something. Callum, if you can get Simone to apologize, then I think you can make friends with anyone."

Chief Walsh cleared his throat and stepped toward them. "Callum, I just wanted to let you know that we've dropped all charges against you."

Callum's mouth dropped open, and he hurried to his feet. "Really? You don't think I did this anymore?"

Ben shook his head beside his father. "No, we found evidence of another computer hacker at the lab during the fire, and it appears Keith Bryant used your ID card to assist the hacker in gaining access to the lab. We also found someone else's DNA in your car with all the sulfur, and we're running it through forensics now. So we'll know their identity shortly."

Running his hands over his face, Callum looked up at the sky with relief. "I don't know what to say except thank you. All of you."

"Well, let's not get too emotional just yet. We've got another fire to clean up here and an arsonist to arrest." The chief stared out onto the scene as firefighters still moved with urgency to keep the forest fire under wraps. "Autumn, a word."

Autumn stood to speak with Chief Walsh separately from the others. "What is it, Chief?"

"We also cleared Alick Carson." The chief lifted his chin toward the fire inspector off in the distance. "He worked another fire at the same time we estimated the university fire occurred, and we also have confirmation of him being at city hall during the inn fire. He didn't do this."

"So, it wasn't Callum or Alick, and we know Keith helped someone get into the lab computers." Autumn thought for a moment. "What do we know about that?"

"Ben?" Chief Walsh called. "What've you got on the computer hacking?"

"We're looking for someone good enough to get into fire-walled systems at the university and access funds and secure information." Ben shrugged and continued. "Whoever it is, they're good, and they know how to cover their tracks. We'll get to Keith Bryant, though, and find out who he's working with."

Autumn quickly put the pieces together and exchanged a knowing look with Lainy. "Someone who knows computers and where to find sulfur at the hot springs . . ."

Lainy nodded along, finishing Autumn's thought. "Because she's ridden with Keith's bike gang."

"Just ridden with them? Or directed their entire operation in the background?" Autumn thought for a moment. "And I'm gonna guess she has long, wavy dark hair and a tattoo of a snake eating its tail."

Gasping and covering her mouth, Lainy nodded. "Yeah, Autumn. She does."

Chapter 24

Autumn made her way to the back of a quiet library the following afternoon and smiled at the nearest librarian.

"Hello, I'm looking for Becca Winsome. Is she working today?"

The older woman at the circulation desk nodded and picked up a telephone. "Yes, I believe she is. Just a moment, please."

Autumn turned slowly to scan the stacks and all the tables around her. Only a few other people walked through the shelves, but she heard some fun being had in the children's area near the front.

"Autumn," a voice called from the double doors at the back wall.

Smiling at seeing her friend from school, Autumn waved and walked over. "Becca, hi. I'm sorry to bother you, but I need some information."

Becca nodded and pushed up her glasses. "Yeah, of course. Do you need access to the genealogy vault downstairs?"

"No, I don't think so." Autumn brought her voice down to a whisper. "This doesn't have anything to do with the founding families, although I can't be sure. I'm looking into someone in particular, though."

"Okay." Becca thought for a moment as she turned to push the double doors open. "Let's go downstairs."

Autumn followed Becca down the winding staircase into the underground genealogy area of the library. Sconces lit the stone walls on either side, and Autumn smiled as Becca brought her back to the same research room she had been to several times before. Becca typed in the code on the modern keypad of the old arched wooden doorway.

Pushing the heavy door open, Becca led the way inside. "All right, what's the name you're looking for?"

"Mairi Wilcox." Autumn pulled her faux leather backpack around to the front of her and began digging around inside. She pulled out the pamphlet from the mountain bike race and pointed to Mairi's name in the list of participants.

"Seriously?" Becca looked at Autumn in confusion. "I just had another patron asking about the same name."

Autumn felt a tinge of worry for a moment, but as she considered it, she knew exactly who the other patron was. "Is this other patron still here, by any chance?"

Becca turned and walked to the door. "Uh, I can check if you'd like." She yanked the door open and peeked across the hall into the glass door of the genealogy office.

Immediately, Autumn saw who she was expecting right inside the office. He looked over at her and sighed before making his way out into the hall.

"Fancy meeting you here," Finn said with a grin.

"Oh, so you two know each other?" Becca questioned as she looked back and forth between them.

"Yeah, thanks, Becca. It sounds like we're looking for the same thing, so I think Finn can help me from here." Autumn gave her a wave. "I appreciate it."

"Okay, well, just come get me across the hall if you need anything." Becca gave Finn a tight-lipped smile and returned to her office.

Finn closed the wooden door to the vault room and turned toward Autumn. "How are you? I heard on the police scanner that you and Lainy got stuck in some kind of forest fire. Are you okay?"

"Oh, yeah, we're both fine. Thanks to Callum." Autumn lifted her eyebrows at the thought.

"Callum McIver? The lab manager we suspected?" Finn sorted through a bunch of file folders on the table.

"Yeah, that Callum. Turns out it's not him behind any of this, but someone tried to make him the scapegoat."

Finn nodded in agreement. "I know. I was wrong about him. Aunt Rose knows his grandfather, and apparently he's a pretty good kid. So since it wasn't him, I did more digging, and I've got some information."

"Let me guess, Mairi Wilcox?" Autumn pulled out a stool from under the large center table, and Finn did the same to sit beside her.

"That's right. I stumbled on her from my research into the mountain bike team. First, I found the team's connections to the fire investigator, who you mentioned met Rowan through them. Then, they all seemed to connect through the university as well. So I followed that until I found the connection with Mairi. How did you know about her?" He pulled a few newspaper clippings out of a file folder.

"Lainy knew Mairi from the computer department at city hall. Mairi apparently also worked at the university for the IT department until recently when she moved to the city job. Plus, I knew she started riding with Rowan's ex on the mountain bike team."

Finn continued Autumn's thoughts. "The university science department has had a string of suspicious computer hacks lately, including around the lab fire time frame. She's got connections there, and she probably knows what information they keep on the system."

"Yep, and I'm pretty sure I saw her at the inn fire, only she acted like she had been there helping people get out rather than starting the fire. I saw a snake tattoo on her arm, too, and Lainy confirmed she has that same tattoo."

"A snake? Snakes symbolize kundalini energy, resurrection, and rebirth." Finn swallowed hard as he connected the dots.

"Yeah, and Lainy and I found a lot of snakes out in the woods by the hot springs. So I'm guessing that's where she's been getting her sulfur for the alchemical process she's plotting." Autumn squinted down at the articles Finn handed to her across the table.

"Autumn, she lost her brother several years back in a fire." Finn pointed to the title of the news article as Autumn read it aloud.

"'Couple Killed in Rare House Fire.'" Autumn scanned the article as Finn continued summarizing it.

"Apparently Mairi's brother died in a fire at his girlfriend's house. They were both killed." Finn sighed and ran a hand through his hair. "But it wasn't an ordinary fire. Even though the article didn't fully explain the cause, it sounded a lot like that fire resulted from an alchemical working gone wrong."

"How do you know that?" Autumn looked from him back to the article, scanning it once again.

"The prime materials found at the scene. Salt, mercury, and sulfur." Finn pointed to a section in the article describing the fire.

"Finn, the girl who died with Mairi's brother . . . her name was Fia McIver. Callum's last name is McIver." Autumn sat for a moment and received a download. "She was Callum's sister."

"That's right. Callum's fire witch, alchemist sister probably caused the fire that killed her and Mairi's brother." Finn crossed his arms and stared at Autumn, waiting for her next logical conclusion.

"So Mairi's still angry and wants revenge for her brother? Fia died in that fire, too, though."

"I think she's still pretty angry, yeah, but I don't think it's revenge she's after, exactly." Finn's eyes went dark as he spoke. "She lost her brother Karter, the only relative she had left." He pointed to the article stating that only Karter's sister, Mairi, survived her brother. "She's got the ire of a thousand armies behind her after losing the one person she had. If something like that happened to me, then all I'd want is to have him back."

"Restitution, then. But he's gone. How can . . ." Autumn squinted at the photo of the burning home and the caption under it that read Fia McIver's name in the description.

Finn nodded in confirmation. "Mmm, now you're on to something. Alchemy has a rule of exchange where you can't gain anything without first giving in return. So is this for restitution? Or perhaps resurrection? I think the snakes are giving us our answer."

Chapter 25

Autumn and Finn rushed to grab copies of the newspaper articles and head out of the library. As soon as they were out front on the sidewalk, Autumn pulled out her phone.

"I'm calling Ben to let him know we suspect Mairi of all this. He'll get someone to track her down." Autumn started messaging him as a call popped up on her phone. "Oh, it's Lainy."

Finn nodded and waited for her to answer. "Maybe she found out more about Mairi."

Autumn answered and immediately felt the stress on the other side of the phone. "Hey, Lainy, what's going on?" She paused for Lainy to speak, and Finn even heard Lainy's hurried tone as he stood across from Autumn. "Okay, slow down. How do you know Anabeth's missing?"

Finn's chest tightened, and he shuffled on his feet as he processed the words. He paced around Autumn, chewing on his lower lip as she finished the conversation.

"Just meet me at Hawthorn Cottage, and we'll figure it out. I'll get Eve and Simone." Autumn hung up and gave Finn a worried look. "Finn, I've gotta go."

"I heard Anabeth's in trouble, so I'm coming with you." Finn headed for his bike chained up on a rack nearby.

"No, you're not. I'm not sure what's going on, and I don't want you getting hurt." Autumn watched as he unlocked his bike and glared at her.

"Autumn, I'll be the judge of whether or not I'm going to get hurt. Anabeth's my friend, and if she's in danger, then I wanna help." He swung a leg over his bike. "Besides, you need me. I know alchemy better than you, or most people, for that matter. If you get in over your head, then you'll need someone who can see through the formulas. And I'm also a pretty good air witch, so there's that." He patted the bike seat behind him. "So we're going to grab Simone and head to your cottage. Do you wanna ride on the seat or the handlebars?"

Sighing, Autumn quickly texted Eve to meet them behind the Pine. They'd all go over to the cottage together to meet Lainy. She threw her leg over the bike seat behind Finn and hoisted herself up onto it as he stood on the pedals. "All right, smooth talker. Let's go."

Finn raced his bike down Havensbrook Place and crossed quickly at Main Street. He stayed in the bike line just barely as he weaved past other bikes. Autumn glanced back at a biker who almost fell off his bike, making sure he was all right.

"He's fine." Finn shrugged it off. "A little adrenaline in his day will do him good."

He pulled the bike up to the front of the Pine and stopped abruptly, almost flinging Autumn off the bike. "Sorry," he said. "Just trying to get us here."

Autumn held on to his shoulder and pulled herself off the bike. She saw Tavish waiting for her inside the front window. His open mouth told her the cat meowed furiously at her inside. "Come on, let's just grab Simone and go."

She flew open the front door with a whirlwind of air around her. A couple customers inside looked up abruptly in surprise, and Simone glanced up from helping a customer with some journals.

"Autumn? What's . . ." Simone tried to get out the words, but Autumn grabbed the journal out of her hands.

"Hello, Mrs. Halpin. It's lovely to see you today, but you'll have to come back later. That journal isn't what you need, anyway." Autumn scurried to the door with her as Simone and Finn stared with wide eyes. "If you come back in two days' time, then I'll have exactly what you need all wrapped up for you, all right?" Autumn nodded and smiled at the mayor's wife and nudged her gently out the door.

"Uh . . ." Simone looked around the shop to see one last customer and took the hint to shoo them out as well. "I'm sorry, but we have to close early today. We'll be open late for the Sun Day Shopping event, though, so be sure to come back for all your paper needs."

The customer nodded in confusion and made their way to the door, and Autumn locked it behind them. She flipped the sign to read Closed and hurried back to Simone and Finn.

"What's going on, cuz? You're freaking me out." Simone looked at Autumn as if she were crazy. "You've got a fiery orange aura, and it's getting redder by the second."

Pulling her cousin by the elbow, Autumn dragged her to the back of the shop. "Anabeth's in trouble. Lainy called and said we should meet her at the cottage to grab the Book of Spells."

Simone eyed Finn for a minute. "And him?" She pointed her thumb at him as he followed behind them.

"He's coming with us," Autumn called as she pushed through the back door. "Tavish! Come on. You're coming, too." The cat ran through the shop, eager to follow his witch. He bounded through the back door in front of them and waited patiently at the door of Simone's SUV.

Simone unlocked the car quickly and shook her head. "Okay, let's go. Everyone in." She started it up quickly as they all piled in. Before she pulled out, someone opened the back passenger door.

"Got room for one more?" Eve questioned.

"Oh, sorry, I forgot to mention Eve's coming, too." Autumn gave her cousin a look. "Now we can go."

"Right." Simone put the car in reverse. "The more the merrier. Although, I don't think that's how this afternoon's gonna go." She drove as fast as she could through the back alley and onto the streets of town, heading for their cottage.

"No, it's not." Autumn shook her head. "We need to be prepared for anything. Lainy mentioned she got a phone call that Anabeth was taken."

"A phone call? From who?" Simone glanced at her curiously.

"I guess now's a good time to mention," Finn interjected from the back seat, "that we know who's behind all of this."

Eve gasped and nodded. "Is it the ex-boyfriend Keith, something or other?" She cocked her head to the side, waiting for his reply.

Finn pointed at Eve definitively. "No, but it is someone in his bike gang. Mairi Wilcox."

"Who's that?" Eve scrunched up her face and looked out the window to watch the tree-lined street as they rounded the corner onto the cottage lane.

"That mountain bike chick Lainy knows from city hall?" Simone opened the center console as she drove and pulled out a small rollerball bottle with essential oils. She held it up to confirm she had the right one. "Frankincense." With a quick glide, she rolled it onto the wrist that held the steering wheel.

Then, she switched hands and rubbed it on the other wrist before giving it to Autumn. "Just a little extra shielding for, you know, whatever."

Autumn nodded and took the bottle. "Good call. We could use all the protection energy we can get." She rolled the essential oil onto her wrists and then handed it to Eve in the back seat.

"Anyway, to answer your question, yes," Autumn continued as they pulled into the driveway at Hawthorn Cottage. "Mairi works at city hall, and Lainy recognized her name at the mountain bike race. We found news articles about her brother dying in a fire, along with Callum's sister, several years back. Finn and I think she's angry enough to seek restitution for her brother dying."

"But he's dead." Eve slammed the car door and got out. "What would she be able to get back?"

Autumn and Finn both sighed and glanced at each other before Autumn answered, "Him, Eve. She wants him back, and she's using alchemy to get him." She noticed Lainy's car already parked in front of the house, and she rushed up the front steps.

Simone jogged up to follow her. "So she's the one piercing the veil and tampering with the worlds."

The door opened abruptly as Lainy stood on the other side, appearing nervous, unlike her usual self. "What took you so long?" She stepped aside for them all to come in. "Finn? What're you doing here?"

"Helping," Finn replied curtly.

Lainy lifted her hands as if giving up and then closed the door behind them. "We don't have much time. Mairi took Anabeth about an hour ago, and if we wanna stop her, then we need the Book of Spells."

"Why?" Eve wondered. "Is there a particular spell that'll undo alchemy or something?"

"Not unless we know exactly what we're undoing." Finn shook his head.

Autumn watched Lainy's jittery hand movements and pacing. This wasn't like Lainy at all, and Autumn wondered what had gotten her so out of balance from her own energy. "Lainy, stop pacing for a moment and look at me."

Lainy swallowed hard and looked straight into Autumn's eyes. "She wants the spell book, Autumn, or she threatened to kill Anabeth."

"What?" Simone yelled. "No way!"

Autumn searched Lainy's eyes, and she saw a determination within them. As Autumn thought for a moment, her attention turned to an open window in the kitchen where the scent of iris flowers drifted through the cottage. She knew right away that Gran was there sending them courage and wisdom.

"It's okay." Autumn walked into the living room. With Gran's presence lingering, she felt a calm come over her. "Let's get the book, and then we'll decide our next steps."

"Gran's here." Simone sensed her grandmother's energy, too, and nodded. "I hope she's giving you some clear guidance on this one, Autumn." She took a deep breath and headed into the living room alongside Autumn.

The others hesitantly followed and grabbed hands. As they linked up in a circle, they closed their eyes.

"Ancestors and elements, we call on you now." Autumn felt the energies swirl around them. "We ask for your help with a friend in danger and the veil being pierced." The kitchen window flew fully open with Autumn's words, and wind furiously swept across the house. "Bring forth the Book of Spells so that we may remove the danger, stop the piercing of the veil, and bring balance back once again."

The bookshelves in the living room rattled in the heavy wind, and the pendant light overhead shook with intensity. Autumn smelled smoky cedarwood in the air, but no candles or fires were lit.

As she opened her eyes, Gran's image stood before her in the living room, holding her hands together at her waist. Autumn looked at Gran in amazement, as she had only ever felt her presence before.

"Be cautious, child," Gran whispered. "Look beyond the surface, and you will do what's right."

Autumn's heart beat faster, and she squeezed Simone's hand beside her. "Wait, Gran."

Having seen Gran also, Simone turned to her cousin. "She believes in you, Autumn, and she's here for you . . . for all of us."

Tears formed in Autumn's eyes. She grabbed at the locket under her shirt, which now pulsed with a gentle warmth. The others opened their eyes to see a brilliant emerald light at Autumn's chest.

"It's glowing, Autumn," Eve said with hurried excitement. "Open it!"

Releasing hands with those beside her, Autumn pulled Gran's locket open to find the tiny key there once again. She lifted it from inside the locket and headed to the wardrobe behind the wall at the front door. "Okay, here we go."

She twisted the key in the wardrobe lock and opened it to find the large wooden chest sitting at the bottom. Autumn bent down to lift the lid and reveal the MacKinnon Book of Spells atop their family flannel. A pang of relief washed over her, but also a hint of worry for what may come.

Simone walked over to Autumn and took the book from her to place it on the coffee table. She flipped it open to the middle. "All right, book. Find us a spell to undo alchemy and rebuild the veil."

The book flipped its pages back and forth wildly as they all watched. It stopped for a moment, only to start up again. Once it slowed and dropped open to a final page, Autumn moved in closer to see it.

"Preservation of Spirit and Raising the Veil." Autumn looked over the spell briefly and saw that it called upon the ancestral spirits without and the spirits within. As she considered it, her eyes went to the open kitchen window just in time to see a vision of a woman's silhouette dart past.

Autumn stepped away from the others, hurrying to the kitchen to peer out. In the distant trees, she spotted Cerridwen looking back at her through a line of smoke.

"Transformation is near." Cerridwen's voice carried through the air.

"Autumn!" Simone jolted her cousin out of the vision. "Are you okay? We haven't closed the circle."

Finn and Eve stood behind her as well, and Autumn rubbed her eyes for a moment to recover.

"Yeah, I just saw something outside." Autumn took a deep breath. "I'm okay now. We can get back to the book and close the circle."

Simone rubbed Autumn's arm and nodded. "Okay, let's go."

Autumn moved between Simone, Eve, and Finn to head back to the living room. But as she did, she felt an emptiness inside of her. Her eyes scanned the room in front of them, only to find the Book of Spells gone and Lainy along with it.

Chapter 26

"We have to go after her! She couldn't have gotten far." Finn grabbed his messenger bag and started waving them all toward the door.

"Hold on," Autumn replied calmly as she stepped slowly toward the coffee table. She squinted down at a napkin with a black ink drawing scribbled on it. "Lainy ran off for a reason."

Simone shook her head. "What reason would make her run off without us? We're a coven."

"Guys, Lainy's a fire witch." Eve pressed her palms down at her sides to calm the energy of the room so everyone would listen. The others turned their gaze to her immediately. She gave them a surprised look in return, as if she hadn't expected that to actually work, but it did. "Right, well, she might have a reason and a small plan, but it's probably a quick one. Fire witches prefer to act spontaneously."

Autumn nodded in agreement. "Eve's right. Lainy's acting on impulse. She knew she needed that Book of Spells to save Anabeth, so she didn't wait around for us to all confer about it. She just grabbed it and ran."

"Ran where?" Finn sighed with frustration and rubbed a hand over his eyes. "It makes no sense for her to go alone when we can all help."

"She's trying to get there first and protect us," Autumn said knowingly, and grabbed the napkin Lainy had left on the coffee table.

Eve put her hands on her hips and sighed with frustration that the others took so long to understand. "Of course she is! This is about her fire magic. She feels responsible and wants to protect us by handling it because she's the fire witch." She shrugged. "I get it. With my earth energy, I always want everyone to feel safe and sound."

They all stared at the napkin as Autumn held it up in the air. A drawing of a snake eating its own tail stood out in the center.

"That's the alchemical symbol for union." Finn tapped his finger on the napkin. "The infamous snake eating its tail represents destruction and rebirth. Moving through difficulty so that you may be born anew and united with all things."

"It's also Mairi's tattoo." Autumn exchanged a serious look with Finn. "She intends that union to happen soon."

Simone squinted at the drawing and watched orange shimmers of magic dancing within the black ink lines on the napkin.

"Lainy left her magic imprinted on that drawing, and it feels pretty darn determined about something." Simone raised her eyebrows at Autumn. "What are you getting from it, cuz?"

"I'm getting that she's putting herself in danger to save everyone herself, but I know where she's headed." Anxiety rushed over Autumn, and she wished the ancestors would speak up to give their insight. "We're gonna need more than just fire energy to get all of them out safely."

"All of them?" Finn watched in confusion as Autumn scrambled to throw a few things into her backpack, including a suspicious-looking vial of something, and headed for the door.

"That's right, all of them," Autumn responded as she simultaneously sent more thoughts to Simone telepathically.

Simone nodded in understanding. "Anabeth, Lainy, and Callum. Salt, mercury, and sulfur." She jogged over to grab her keys from the tiny shelf by the front door.

"Triple goddess! What are we getting into?" Finn ran his fingers through his brown hair and intertwined them at the back of his head.

Autumn paused after pulling open the front door. "Triple goddess?" She eyed Finn for a moment. "You're referring to Cerridwen."

Finn nodded and walked out to the front porch as Eve and Simone followed. "Yeah, it's just something I say since growing up around alchemy and elemental magic. Cerridwen brings about transformation, and that's what comprises alchemy."

Autumn locked the door behind them while Simone fired up the car engine. "I've been hearing that a lot lately."

They all hopped into Simone's SUV before she ran over the grass in the front yard heading out. "I'm assuming you know where we're going?" She looked over at Autumn in the passenger seat.

"I sure do." Autumn lifted an eyebrow and tilted her head to one side. "And Cerridwen awaits."

Simone studied the dusty bike trail leading into the woods in front of her, where Autumn and Lainy had found the hot springs. A haze of deep red lifted from the earth onto the trail.

"Well, this looks delightful." She rolled her eyes before taking a deep breath to psych herself up for what lay ahead.

"I see it, too." Autumn nodded. "The red haze . . . It's the earth trying to protect itself from harm."

"I guess we'd better protect ourselves as well, then." Simone headed to the back of the SUV and rummaged through some supplies. She popped open a floor hatch in the trunk and lifted out a couple black tourmaline crystal bracelets, which she strung onto both her wrists. Next, she grabbed a pocket-sized mirror and tucked it into the back of her skinny jeans before nodding. "We've got this."

Autumn, Eve, and Finn met her at the trunk, each putting their cell phones and a few of their own magical items into their pockets.

Simone pushed a flannel blanket aside to make room for their bags, and a meow quickly followed. She raised an eyebrow and flipped over the blanket to reveal a tiny stowaway.

"Tav!" Autumn scooped up the cat and gave his head a kiss. "Thanks for coming along, little guy, but the rocky land out here may be rough on your paws. You need to be careful if you're gonna go out there, okay?" Tavish meowed and purred back at his witch. "All right, then." She dropped him down to the ground beside her and walked to the beginning of the trailhead, where a familiar object caught her eye.

She bent down and grabbed a half-empty mango juice cup off a log on the side of the trail. Lifting it in the air, Autumn sighed. "Looks like Callum is here after all." She tossed the cup into a nearby trash barrel and brushed off her hands. "I guess he didn't have time to finish his drink before someone else showed up."

"Mairi. What's the plan?" Finn asked with worry in his voice.

Autumn grabbed his forearms and smiled. "Finn, I know you like plans just as much as I do, but we're gonna need a certain amount of fast thinking today if we're gonna deal with this fire energy. Can you handle that?"

Finn paused for a moment to consider Autumn's words. "Yeah, I can do that, but . . . do we at least have a starting point to work from here?"

"Breathing always works." Eve chuckled. "If you get into trouble, just breathe and know that we're all here to help."

"That's right. Just use your magic if necessary and trust yourself," Autumn agreed. She rubbed Finn's forearms and took a few deep breaths with him. "We're going to get them back because we're powerful witches and the ancestors and elements have our backs." She looked him straight in the eyes and willed her words into his mind just as much as her own. "We're powerful witches."

Nodding repeatedly, he gave her a slight grin. "We're powerful witches. We can do this." He took another deep breath. "I'm good. Let's do this."

Simone quietly closed the trunk and swirled her finger in the air to signal them to head out. "You take the lead, cuz. You've been here before."

Autumn drew her attention to the tree line and took in a breath. She felt the humming of the mountain jays within the trees, the soft quaking of aspen leaves rippling through the forest, and the deep warmth of the hot sulfur resting beneath travertine rocks. With that warmth, she also sensed the fear surrounding it.

"Mairi's waiting for us near the hot springs." Autumn started through the trees as the others followed her at a quick pace. "She wants us deep into the forest at the source of her alchemical power."

"The sulfur," Simone said as she hopped over a few tree roots.

"That's right, the sulfur." Autumn moved under tree branches easily and glided through the forest as if there were no obstacles whatsoever. She watched the signs of the forest and whispered under her breath, "Ancestors and elements, hear my call. Guide us to reclaim the ones taken from us and reinstate the veil. Let none pass across it that does not belong. Send us the energy for what must be done."

"Autumn." Simone leaned closer to her cousin at the front of the line. "The strawberry moon rises higher in the sky. We might only have another half hour of daylight."

Turning to acknowledge Simone's comment, Autumn nodded. "I hear you." She watched the glints of sunlight beginning to hide below the tree line. The next morning would mark the longest day of sunlight for the year. "Mairi's using this evening to activate the final alchemical process. That way it'll take its full effect as the sun rises on the solstice morning. We can't let her finish it."

Tavish trampled a few leaves as he bounded ahead of Autumn. He stopped below a tree next to the path and waited for her to see it.

"I know, Tav. I've seen the markings." Autumn came up to the tree and traced a finger through the protection eye symbol she and Lainy had found on their previous visit here. "We're getting close." She scanned the tree canopy above. "Ancestors, have you heard my call?"

Autumn and Tavish stared at one another, waiting for a reply, when the screech of an owl echoed loudly through the trees, bringing their attention upward again. She watched as its white outstretched wings glided above with perfect ease before closing to land on a nearby pine tree.

"Oh, Autumn, that's your spirit animal." Eve put her hands on her hips and smiled. "So that's a good sign." Staying chipper, she walked up toward the others at the marked tree.

Autumn focused her mind and sent a message into the wind. "Thank you, ancestors. I will not doubt your presence here again." She shook off the uneasiness she had been keeping to herself and focused on the others. "The owl brings us a very good sign. The ancestors are with us, and we're ready to reset the balance of energy." She pointed to the symbol on the tree. "The bike gang used this protection symbol for their own gain, but we're reclaiming this land now."

Placing her palm flat against the tree, Autumn sent golden shimmering waves of energy into it. Eve moved beside her and clasped Autumn's other hand to add more energy.

"The land knows we're here to support it. No longer shall it be beholden to another's malicious intentions." Autumn continued forward, following the symbols on the trees toward the rockier ground. The earth below her feet shimmered with warm yellow sparks, verifying its new sense of strength.

As Autumn moved over larger rocks now, the locket against her chest quickly warmed. It vibrated with an intensity that she had become accustomed to over the past year of mysterious dealings. "Stay on your toes from here on out. And Sim?"

Simone tapped her temple and gave Autumn a wink. "Gotcha. I'm texting Ben our location now."

Tavish led the way, bounding over several boulders with just as much playfulness as determination. Gran's locket almost burned against Autumn's skin now as Tavish took one last bound and halted. Autumn knew instantly that the hot springs sat directly in front of them.

Simone, Finn, and Eve stood behind Autumn as she paused on the horizon of an expansive rock line. Simone watched as her cousin's silhouette radiated a bright orange glow against the backdrop of a twilight sky.

"Embrace the dark ahead, Autumn, so you can unite it with the light," Simone called out to her.

Autumn twisted her head around to look back at her cousin. She recalled the words her father had said to her in the stone circle vision. "Unite the worlds within so you can unite the worlds without." She repeated them out loud and took a breath. "Ancestors, give me the strength to understand my path." With the words, she and Tavish took a few more steps forward and vanished below the horizon.

The three others exchanged a worried glance before rushing ahead to the rock line themselves. As they stared down the rocky hill before them, they watched Autumn and Tavish float around huge turquoise hot spring pools.

Eve's mouth dropped open as she scanned the landscape of beautiful bubbling waters and travertine stones. "This is incredible."

Simone's intuition quickly guided her focus to the far end of the pools where Autumn and Tavish headed. Before them in the distance stood three silhouettes in the middle of a massive hand-drawn dirt circle with a pentacle in its center. A cauldron furiously bubbled away alongside them, and along with it, a serpent poised to strike.

Chapter 27

Lainy, Anabeth, and Callum stood eerily still within the large transmutation circle. The pentagram inscribed within it looked exactly like Arailt had described as the last sign of the alchemical process. That meant Mairi grew close to completing her intention.

The sounds of the bubbling cauldron and spurting hot springs broke through the heaviness in the air, and Autumn's heart beat so fast she thought it would leap out of her chest.

She swallowed hard and locked eyes with Lainy, who mouthed, *I'm sorry*, from across the terrain. Giving her a tight-lipped smile, Autumn nodded in forgiveness.

She moved closer as Simone, Eve, and Finn came up behind her. Taking a step to cross the threshold of the circle, Autumn jumped back as huge flames sprang up and ran along the entire perimeter.

Simone pulled her back and watched the flames dance before leaning over to her cousin's ear. "This is about control. The alchemist holds no actual connection to the elements." Always sensing the aura of things, Simone interpreted the world by feeling, and right now, she felt only a domineering power over this fire rather than one of respect.

Autumn understood and moved around the perimeter of the circle in a clockwise direction as everyone's eyes followed her movement. She took in every detail of the scene. The cauldron bubbled with an effervescent purple liquid, and beside it stood a tall stand with a clamp. On the ground the serpent continued to bob its head back and forth, eyeing the three captives with every motion. Behind it, the MacKinnon Book of Spells was splayed out on the ground, along with a small wooden box with the same snake eating its tail that Autumn had seen on Mairi's shoulder.

On each point of the hand-drawn pentagram, a small circle covered the tip. Palm-sized stones lay on the three topmost points, with alchemical symbols for salt, mercury, and sulfur carved into them. Autumn assumed Mairi had intentionally placed them there to merge the three primes in the alchemical process.

With dusk setting in, the glowing fire circle danced through a gentle breeze, and a deep cackle sounded in the distant trees. A tall figure with long brown hair over her bare shoulders, revealing the snake tattoo, appeared.

"Well, here we are at last." Mairi stepped out of the dark tree line and closer to the fiery transmutation circle.

Autumn spotted a large round flask in Mairi's hand. She thought about the contents of her own backpack and knew the vial she'd received from Arailt remained tucked in the side pocket.

"I guess you all know who I am by now." Mairi smiled. "Lainy's known me for a while now, and I've done my homework on all of you." She tipped the flask back and forth between her fingers as she spoke, letting the contents churn with a deep-purple spiral mixing within it. "Let's see. Autumn's the head of your little coven, and then we have Simone, the activist, Eve, the pastry chef, and Finn, Anabeth's protégé. Did I miss anyone?"

Tavish hissed at Mairi's words and clawed at the air in her direction.

"Oh, you brought a little cat friend as well." Mairi moved to the eastern edge of the circle. "Isn't that so predictable of you, witches?"

"Mairi, we know you lost your brother. It's a terrible thing to lose someone, let alone the only family you have. But carrying anger toward Callum and his sister won't fix anything. And it certainly won't help to hurt others because your own heart is broken. They've done nothing." Autumn pointed at Anabeth and felt Mairi's anger spark in that moment.

"What do you know about any of it?" Mairi spattered back. "You're all just like that witch, Fia, who killed my brother with her alchemical magic. I told Karter she was bad for him, but he didn't listen. He said he loved her for who she was, and look where that got him. Ten feet in the grave! And then that nosy one Rowan meddled in things that didn't concern her while I ran my experiments at the lab. That's why I confused her with those drawings and pointed everything to Callum so he'd take the blame."

"You made those drawings for Rowan, and Keith gave them to her." Autumn finally understood that Keith had always been just a middleman.

"Of course I did. Keith's useless except for some things, but he'll follow along if there's something in it for him. He doesn't matter, though. I have bigger plans for my brother and me, and now that I have the funds to accomplish them, well, I just need my brother by my side."

Finn and Simone shifted around the left side of Mairi, but she darted her gaze over to them.

"Ah, ah, ah. Not so fast!" Mairi held the flask higher for them all to see. With her other hand, she grabbed for a particular stone that appeared to be wet with some kind of substance all over it. Throwing it onto the fire circle, the stone put out a small section of the flames, and she walked over it into the circle center. She pulled the stone back through the center along with her. "You wouldn't want me to pour this little vial into that cauldron over there, because if I did, well . . ." She made a tsking sound with her tongue. "Let's just say there would be no more hot springs around here and none of us either."

"I know it's difficult, but you can move on, Mairi. You're not going to bring him back." Autumn tuned into Mairi's thoughts, and she perceived a break in the veil.

Mairi made a few preparations in the center of the circle. She barked back at Autumn, "I am bringing my brother back! And you're going to help me." She moved the wet stone toward Autumn at the north end of the circle. "Come here and don't even think about using your magic." She shook the flask within her fingers again as she waited for Autumn.

Through the haze of smoke, Autumn spotted Cerridwen trailed by another more familiar face on the far side. Her necklace glowed brightly with green, and she smelled cedarwood in the air as her gran smiled back at her by Cerridwen's side.

Simone followed Autumn's gaze as it went right past her, and she instantly felt the energy from their grandmother nearby. It felt like a warm breeze wrapping her in an embrace. She turned to Autumn and telepathically sent her a message. *Just say the word, and we'll end this.*

Stepping onto the stone Mairi had positioned, Autumn calmly crossed the fire circle into the middle. She sent Simone a message back through her mind. *Go to your spot on the circle, but do not use Mairi's pentacle as your guide. We're claiming*

*the circle as our own to overpower it, and we need Eve and Finn
to move in kind.*

Simone tapped a finger to the side of her nose to signal her understanding, and she slowly inched closer to the western point, where water usually presided over a witch's circle.

Autumn let out a powerful breath and called to the fire as she continued closer to Mairi and the captives in the middle. "Fire within me, converge with the roaring fire of this circle." She spoke to it in her mind as a flame rose on the far side and listened intently to the fae witch before it. "Banish the grip held over you and regain your own will. As I speak, may you come more into balance within and without."

The fire tamed around the entire circle, and Mairi spun around quickly to watch it. "I told you no magic!" She stepped quickly over to the bubbly cauldron and held the flask over it, pouring one drop into it. A burst of a purple bubbly substance popped from within it and spurted out a few feet away.

Finn covered his face with his hand at the east and murmured, "Double, double toil and trouble." All eyes moved to him, stopping the unfoldment for a moment. He threw his hands up, showing he wasn't trying anything. "Shakespeare, only Shakespeare."

Mairi's face grew stern. "Don't test me, any of you. Now, Autumn, grab that book and read."

As Autumn bent to retrieve the Book of Spells from the ground, the serpent backed down slowly to allow it. Simone motioned to Eve and Finn when Mairi wasn't looking, and they each moved to their respective positions on the circle.

Eve took a breath to center herself at the northern point. She gave Lainy a look at the center, and Lainy knew instantly to move a few steps toward the south.

At the east, Finn discreetly put his hand deep into his front pocket and latched on to a thin silver wand he had brought. He kept it hidden from view but pulled it toward the top of his pocket for easier access.

Oblivious to their motives, Mairi focused on the Book of Spells that Autumn now held. She hovered the flask over the cauldron to maintain a sense of control. "You're going to read the spell and finish the coagulation process for me." Mairi laughed and looked down at the small wooden box on the ground. "What better way to reverse my brother's fiery death at the hands of an alchemical witch than by returning him to me with alchemy and a witch's words?"

Autumn eyed the box in realization. Her pulse quickened as she traced the snake symbol on the box.

Mairi bent down and met Autumn's eyes. "That's right. My brother's ashes rest in that box. Open it and pour them onto the ground." She watched as Autumn hesitantly did as Mairi told her. "We shall soon have our union, brother. But hopefully your affinity toward trusting witches like Fia won't return with you."

"You shut up about my sister!" Callum yelled, unable to stand by and allow Mairi to disparage the sibling he'd lost. "She was a good person and never meant your brother harm."

"Don't speak to me about being a good person! You know nothing!" Mairi moved back over to the cauldron. "You're an alchemical witch just like her, and you're gonna take the fall for this, Callum. It's a good thing I learned alchemy in secret over the years so I could give it all right back to you. Of course, no one would teach a natural-born such as myself. That's where working on the university computers for years came in handy. It wasn't hard to come by the information I needed. Once I learned enough, the time came to begin the process, and now I'm ready to finish this once and for all."

"Mairi, the police know Callum isn't at fault. They know you marked him, and they're on their way." Autumn ran her hand down the page of the Book of Spells, imbuing it with her energy once again.

"Just read the spell on the page!" Mairi yelled, more nervous now than she had been all evening.

Autumn gazed down through the dim light of the now-risen strawberry moon. "Wall between the worlds, hear my call." She swallowed deeply and let the book feel her touch, knowing it had strong ancestral energy within it.

"Keep going. Word for word, witch." Mairi poured another drop into the oozing cauldron and kept an eye on all of them.

"Pierce the veil and converge the taken spirit with matter once again." Autumn slowed down her words as she looked ahead in the spell. While quite long, clear signs would make the spell's progress evident to Mairi as Autumn proceeded. If she wanted to change the spell, she would need to be clever about it. She pieced a plan as she continued, "Make the equivalent exchange. Matter for matter. Spirit for spirit."

Anabeth grabbed at her stomach in the center of the circle, dropping to the ground, writhing. Finn anxiously inched his wand out of his pocket a bit and tried crossing the circle into the center. Flames rose slightly around the outer line, and Simone gave him a stern look to stop.

Finn watched Autumn stand still on the spot, looking straight down at Anabeth as if silently performing her own spell in her mind. He anxiously eyed them both until something caught his attention on the ground. The rocky earth below Karter's ashes sizzled with heat as a fissure formed and allowed a thick purple liquid to bubble through it.

Autumn stepped back, along with Callum, as Mairi widened her eyes with anticipation at the sight. The sizzling turned into spurting purple molten lava and something taking shape within the ground.

Nodding with contentment, Mairi lowered the flask. "The coagulation has begun."

Chapter 28

Autumn watched the ground under Karter's ashes bubble and take shape into something she didn't want to go any further. Tavish found a way into the heart of the transmutation circle and brushed up against her leg. She smiled down at the cat, knowing the time had come to put an end to this madness.

With a quick intention, Autumn blew a soft breath into the breeze, allowing it to land on the cat's ear below her. Tavish perked up and meowed at her, knowing instantly that his witch wanted him to go find help.

While Tavish ran toward the wooded path, Autumn placed her hand over the pages of the Book of Spells, and they shimmered under her touch. Focusing her energy, she called for the spell the girls had pulled open previously at the house. The current page instantly melted into the others and disappeared. Words rearranged themselves to transform into the spell from earlier in the cottage: Preservation of Spirit and Raising the Veil.

Swallowing hard and switching to the new spell, Autumn hoped Mairi would be none the wiser. She took a step closer to the bubbling ground, but Callum pulled on her sleeve.

"Autumn, don't," Callum whispered.

She gave him a calming face and whispered back, "It's okay." Then, she winked.

Stunned by her confidence, Callum watched the ground in front of her.

"We embrace the ancestors who came before us and remain within us." Autumn's voice drew the attention of Finn and the coven members around the edge of the circle. They listened carefully and watched golden shimmers of light appearing from the Book of Spells.

Mairi stood in her spot, oblivious to the elemental magic at hand, but prodding Autumn still. "Keep going! The spell is working!"

Not wanting to drag this on, Autumn continued with her own spell. "We call upon you to preserve body, mind, and spirit within their realms." Her pace quickened now, as she knew

Mairi would catch on fast. "Raise the veil once more and deny any who may try to pass. Maintain the balance of our worlds."

The winds picked up around them and maintained the force of a raging storm. Eve nodded at Simone, Finn, and Lainy across the circle, and they raised their palms at their sides, directing the energies of earth, air, fire, and water. Clouds formed in the dark sky overhead, and drops trickled down over the flaming circle, which quieted its rage and eased toward the ground. Rocky dirt kicked up in the wind and extinguished the final flames. The serpent in the center of the circle cowered in disgust of the rain, looking for a place to hide.

"What are you doing?" Mairi yelled. She raced over to the cauldron and poured a drop from the flask into it while wiping away the rain from her face. Huge bursts of fire flew out of the cauldron, and Mairi threatened to do it again. "Get back to my spell!"

Autumn disregarded Mairi's words as Cerridwen captivated her in the distance. The crone walked calmly through the pounding rain and smiled softly. Gran and several other ancestors stood at the tree line, watching as well.

Gran blew a kiss into the wind and whispered, "You know who you are, Autumn. You no longer need the old ways to guide you. Trust your magic, and we will remain with you on your path."

Autumn looked between each of the coven members and knew what she had to do to end this. She put her hand over

Gran's locket at her chest and nodded. "You're all within me. I know that now."

She grabbed the vial from the side pocket of her backpack. Popping the cork from the top with her fingers, she poured the contents onto the ground where the ashes began their transformation into flesh.

Mairi's eyes widened as she watched the ground flatten out again. "No, the spell worked! You can't stop it!" She lunged at Autumn and the Book of Spells.

At lightning speed, Lainy bolted across the circle toward them and kicked up her foot directly into Mairi's abdomen, sending her flying back onto the ground with force.

Surprised, Mairi fumbled on the ground, and Autumn took the opportunity to say the final words of the spell. "With my words, the worlds remain intact. In mind, body, and spirit, none shall pass without the proper time. As I say it, so shall it be."

She blew firmly into her palm, igniting a strong flame, even through the pouring rain. Gulping down the second thoughts of what she was about to do, Autumn brought the flame of her palm toward the edge of the Book of Spells. The pages ignited instantly, and a tall column of fire rose as she dropped the book to the ground.

Mairi dove for the book, crying and using her wet shirt to tamp the flames. It was no use, though. The book had already burned halfway through and lay on the rocky ground flaming but also covered in pounding rain.

Autumn turned to Finn. "Can you handle that cauldron?"

He nodded and yanked the silver wand from his pocket where he'd been grasping it at the ready. "I've got it. I know what to do."

"Lainy!" Autumn called her over to where Mairi knelt over the burning book, shaking in the rain with the cowering serpent beside her. Autumn and Lainy raised their palms to their sides and summoned their fire energy. "Fire within us, rein in the dark. Encircle the one who intends harm. Bring no one through your flames until my words make it so."

Nodding at Autumn, Lainy swept her hand across the air in the shape of a circle. Flames rose off the ground around Mairi, who was still attempting to put out the fire engulfing the book and shield it from the other elements.

"Like for like. The way of the alchemist, isn't it?" Lainy glared down at her and then turned her back.

Simone wrapped her arm around Anabeth at the south end of the circle as she whispered to the rain. "Calm the water. Save it for another day."

The rain slowly dissipated, and Anabeth looked up at the sky with relief. She sighed with exhaustion. "Is it over?"

"Almost, Anabeth, almost." Simone watched the north end of the circle as Callum intertwined his alchemical knowledge with Finn's at the cauldron.

The two of them grabbed handfuls of the rocky dirt and dropped them into the iron pot. Eve hurried to gather the stones carved with alchemical symbols at each of the destroyed pentagram points. She ran back to the cauldron and threw them in as well.

"We could use a bit of fire over here when you get a chance." Finn waved Autumn and Lainy toward the cauldron.

They moved to a position opposite Finn and Callum and firmly planted themselves, hovering their hands high above the pot. As they did so, the cauldron liquid came to a roiling boil with hues of purple, blue, and green.

Finn raised his wand and swirled it in a clockwise motion. "Elements of earth, air, fire, and water, you have been improperly summoned. Dissipate this energy. Remove the toxins and transmute them into something pure. As the air within me cleanses, so, too, does the air that exists here. Cleanse and dissipate. Cleanse and dissipate. Cleanse and dissipate."

He lifted his wand, and a gentle breeze glided down softly into the cauldron. Looking up to Autumn, he nodded. "Help me with the final step?"

She nodded, and they used the edges of their shirts to take hold of the still-hot cauldron handles. On either side, the two of them turned it over onto the ground where Karter's ashes had bubbled. The contents seeped into the earth, pulling the ashes down with it to rebalance once again.

"Salt, mercury, and sulfur of the earth. Go back to it as you must." Finn pointed his wand down at the wet ground.

"Elements, balance and take your proper place." Autumn closed her eyes and envisioned the cauldron's contents transmuting to create new life on this same spot. "And so it is."

When Autumn opened her eyes, Lainy stood in front of her, tearing up. "Autumn, I'm so sorry for taking the Book of Spells. Mairi threatened to kill Callum and Anabeth if I didn't come alone, and I didn't want any of you in danger either."

Mairi still knelt, defeated, on the wet ground with the burned book a blackened crisp beside her. Flames remained high around her, but Autumn sensed the intense despair she had.

Autumn sighed and met eyes with Lainy. "It's not your fault, Lainy. Your intentions were good. So you made a decision and acted on what you knew in the moment. Plus"—she shook her head in amazement—"I don't know how I could be mad when you pulled out that powerhouse kick and bought me some time."

Lainy laughed and put her hands on her hips. "Yeah, who knew those martial arts classes would lead to some deep-rooted strength of mine?"

Smiling with relief, Autumn scanned the scene before finding Cerridwen standing under the light of the strawberry moon in the distant trees. She stood with Gran and a long line of ancestors. The crone nodded to Autumn before transforming into a black raven and flying over the tree line.

Gran stepped forward and gave Autumn a smile. "It's time to let us go, my sweet girl. You know the path ahead, and we'll always be with you, even without the words in a book. Just remember that a four-points witch never doubts herself, and you proved that to yourself today. You took hold of your inner world, knowing that you had everything you needed all along. And you took hold of the world outside as well by not allowing it to overcome that inner truth. So do not mourn the Book of Spells, for it was a thing of the past. Now you must create your own future . . . with the coven, of course."

Gran blew another kiss into the wind, and Autumn followed its trailing light through the air before landing on her cheek. It warmed her skin like a summer afternoon, and she raised her hand to touch her cheek with contentment.

Turning to the others gathered around her, Autumn heard calls of the police approaching in the distance. "Tonight showed us who we are and where we came from, and from now on, we don't look back . . . only forward."

Chapter 29

Simone dragged herself through the back door of Parchment and Pine the following morning, bright and early, with Autumn behind her. She slowly pulled the round Lennon sunglasses from her eyes and raked a hand through her hair.

"I can't believe we have to be here all day today after the night we had!" Simone tossed her things under the counter and went into the back office to sort through the music selection. She found some Pat Benatar and cranked it over the speakers. "That's better."

Autumn sighed at the music choice and rolled the beads of her green aventurine bracelet between her fingers to gain a little peace. When she felt ready to face the tasks at hand, she grabbed a bunch of boxes from the back office. "I know it was a rough night, but this is a big day. We can't let Main Street down. We're always a big draw for the Sun Day event, and this'll give us a nice boost of funds until the holiday season hits. That's why I asked for a little help with decorating this morning." She smirked at her cousin.

"Help, you say? Bless you!" Simone put her hands together in a prayer position and followed Autumn onto the shop floor, grabbing a few items Autumn dropped here and there. "I really hope whoever you messaged brings coffee. Then they'll really be our saviors."

The music amped up, and the girls pulled decorations from a large cardboard box marked "Sun Day." Tavish paced back and forth at the front door before one of his favorite people knocked on the glass. He meowed at Autumn as if requesting her to answer it quickly.

She laughed at the cat and came over to unlock it. "Okay, Tav. I'll let him in."

The antique bell chimed above the door as James walked inside, with Ben trailing close behind him. James leaned over and kissed Autumn. "Hey, how are you?"

Tavish stretched his paws up James's leg and meowed for attention. Shaking her head at the cat, Autumn focused back on James. "I'm good, thanks. Just glad to see you." She dipped her head back to wave at Ben. "Hey, Ben. Thanks for coming this morning, guys."

James crouched down to give Tavish his much-needed attention. "Thanks for asking us to come. I got worried after Ben told me what happened last night."

Simone ran up to Ben as soon as she saw him carrying a tray full of hot drinks from the Forest Brew. "You are my savior!" She snatched a drink off the tray and started sipping on it.

Ben smirked and watched her drink it down. "I like the sound of that." He took the opportunity to give her a quick kiss when she came up for air from the drink.

She gave him a glare and then went back to drinking. "Did you get any sleep after last night?"

Ben sighed and walked the rest of the drinks to the back counter. "No, I couldn't sleep. After we got the scene processed and took Ms. Wilcox to lockup, it was well into the morning hours. I couldn't calm my mind down after that, and I just wanted to check up on you. So I'm glad Autumn texted."

"Yes! We need both of your help to get this place looking good for the Sun Day Shopping today." Autumn handed a long string of fairy lights to James. "The doors open in a couple hours, and we have a lot to do. I've got tons of fairy lights, mason jar lights, and lots of candles, which will be under my magical supervision the whole day. So if you guys could grab a ladder from the back and start hanging lights, that would be great."

James nodded to Ben. "Okay, we're on it."

Simone angled her thumb toward the far wall. "I'll prep the fire in the hearth room if you wanna fix the front window display."

Autumn headed that way. "Yeah, sounds good. Karen Leslie's coming over from next door, anyway. She's gonna bring us a bunch of fresh sunflowers from the flower shop, so I'll grab those when she comes."

Pulling a few suncatchers from a side display, Autumn moved a stand closer to the middle of the front window. She hung the suncatchers prominently on the stand and smiled as they shimmered in the morning sun. Then, she draped long strands of green velvet ribbons from the ceiling at different lengths in the window. She grabbed a few paper daisy wreaths and wrapped them by the ribbons to give a dainty wildflower look to the scene. The entire window display looked like a blooming summer meadow, and it would overflow with even more color after a few flower bouquets arrived from Karen.

At the thought of it, Autumn heard Karen Leslie knocking on the front door and peering inside. She quickly opened it to find Karen adjusting an armload of tall sunflower stalks.

"Morning, love! It's a beautiful day to be a shop owner." She placed the giant bouquet in Autumn's arms.

"You're right, Karen. It is." Autumn waved Simone to come help. "How's the flower shop coming? Are you ready for a big day of customers?"

Simone brought two massive bell-shaped glass vases to the front and set them down on the platform in the front window.

Autumn and Karen arranged several stalks of sunflowers in each one.

"We're just about ready, yes." Karen paused for a moment. "You know, after you girls and my Quinn recommended I hire help, I found someone from the university. Her name's Olivia, and she's just lovely! I think she's a horticulture major."

"Oh, that's amazing, Karen." Autumn gave her a hug. "I'm so happy that you have help to keep the shop going. You know we miss Mr. Leslie, but we didn't wanna lose you around here, too."

Karen grasped Autumn's hands. "Thank you, dear. I miss him so much, but the shop keeps me going. Main Street has always been a part of who I am, and you girls have become a large part of that as well." Tears formed in her eyes. "Oh, now!" She waved a hand through the air. "I need to get back to the shop and finish my own display. You girls have a wonderful day, all right? I hope you make lots of sales!" She made her way to the front and out the door.

Simone eyed her cousin while she rolled the velvet ribbon back onto the spool. "You're pretty good at focusing on everyone else's needs. Anyone else wouldn't suspect a thing, but I know you, cuz."

Autumn squinted at her cousin. "What're you talking about?"

Simone sighed and rolled her eyes. "I mean, you're trying to be there for Karen and also keep everything together for today's event. Yet, you haven't said one word about the book or what you saw last night that made you burn it. I know it's eating at you."

"Oh, that." Autumn fixed a few sunflower stalks and readjusted the vase's position in the window.

"Yes, oh, that." Simone slid onto the window platform and gave her cousin a continuous stare. "Well? Are you gonna finally tell me what happened?"

Autumn glanced back at the guys busy hanging mason jar lights around the ceiling. "What do you want me to say?" She shrugged and sank down onto the platform beside Simone. "Cerridwen came to me, along with Gran and the ancestors." She swallowed hard. "They told me it was time to let go, to stop doubting myself, and to just move forward."

"So you went all in, Lainy style, and your first reaction led to burning the book?" Simone nodded and continued sarcastically. "Sensible."

Autumn shoved her cousin with her shoulder. "Stop." She sighed and admitted, "I'm sad to have lost the Book of Spells, and I'm really sorry that I had to burn it. I know it wasn't only mine."

Simone grabbed her cousin's shoulders in her hands and turned Autumn to face her directly. "I'm not asking you to apologize. You did what you had to do, and it sounds like the ancestors and Gran knew you had to do it." She shook her head and widened her eyes. "It's just a book. Our coven is the important part, and we all survived. But I know you replay things over and over in your mind, so I wanna make sure you're not beating yourself up about it. Just let it go." She wrapped her arms around Autumn and let out a deep breath.

"Thanks, Sim." Autumn pulled a knee up onto the platform and thought for a moment. "You know, I'm actually okay with my decision to burn the book. I mean, I'm not thrilled to have lost all our family spells, but . . . it's a new beginning, and we can finally look ahead just like I said last night. For some reason, we needed to get rid of the old ways to do it, but it feels right somehow."

Nodding, Simone agreed with her cousin. "Yeah, I hear you. Those spells were someone else's workings. The ancestors before us. So it does feel pretty freeing that we can now work as a coven with fresh energy."

"Yeah, fresh energy." Autumn smiled and looked around the shop. "I like that a lot. We should celebrate tonight at our moms' house for the solstice."

Simone's eyes widened. "Oh, I have something for you tonight! Don't let me forget to give it to you."

"You do?" Autumn gave her cousin an inquisitive sideways look. "I guess I'm getting better with surprises these days."

"Yeah, you are! I'm very impressed with how much you've been going with the flow and being more spontaneous." Simone intertwined her arm into Autumn's. "Now, come on. We've got a Sun Day event to put on! I'll grab the A-frame sign and put it out front. Half off our suncatchers and floral wreaths?"

"Sounds good, thanks." Autumn headed to the center tables next to fix a stand of shimmering crystals that caught the light around their tissue papers. She ran her hand over the stand that once held the black tourmaline pendant. "Anabeth."

A chime sounded at the front door, and Simone held it open for Anabeth to walk in. Smiling as she held up the same pendant that Autumn had given her days ago, Anabeth walked it back to the center display.

"I thought it would be best if I returned this now." Anabeth hugged Autumn and whispered, "Thank you for everything."

"It was nothing." Autumn shook her head and let out a laugh. She pulled a cloth from one of the cardboard boxes and polished the black tourmaline before hanging it back on the display. "I'm glad this gave you the protection you needed."

"Now someone else can put it to good use." Anabeth headed for the door again. "I'll try to come back after I've reviewed Finn's story and submitted my article on the downtown revitalization. James, thanks for helping with that, by the way. It gave me a good distraction from everything else." With a wave, she headed back out to Main Street.

Autumn felt her confidence reemerging with everything getting back to normal. This was going to be a great Sun Day and an even better solstice.

She watched the guys finish the lights and felt the gratitude for their support sweep over her. "James, that was nice of you to help Anabeth with the story."

James stepped down from the ladder as Ben held the bottom. "Yeah, well, I had some time open up in my calendar." He smirked.

"Uh-huh." Autumn put her hands on her hips and admired the shop coming together. "Hey, it looks great in here! Need any more help?"

"Nope, we're done with these. Just give us the next job, boss." James crossed his arms while he waited for Autumn to reply.

She paused for a moment to receive a download. "Actually, Ben, my mom's on her way over with something special for you, Mr. New Sheriff." Autumn pointed to the front door. "There she is now." Turning to James, she threaded her fingers between his. "As for you, Mr. Fix-it, come with me." She led him into the hearth room where the fire now blazed. Wrapping her arms around his neck, she sighed. "I'm sorry I said I needed some space."

James nodded and brushed her hair from her eyes. "Mmm, well, how did that work out for you?"

Autumn looked into the fire. "Challenging." She shrugged and returned her eyes to his. "Turns out what I was looking for in my father and my ancestors has been right here all along. I don't need anything else but what I already have."

Smiling, he moved closer into her aura. "And what's that?"

"Contentment." Autumn pressed up on her tiptoes and met his lips. "One owl, one raven." She tilted her head and glanced to the shop floor where Simone and her mother gave

Ben a small kraft paper tea bag with golden shimmers seeping from the edges. "And the support of a coven that I love by my side."

Chapter 30

Autumn stood over the large black cauldron in the center of Jo's back garden. It had been a long couple of days, and she felt the need to recharge her energy. After a full but successful Sun Day at the shop, all she wanted to do was unwind with the coven and soak in a little garden magic.

She raised her palms over the caldron and took a deep breath. "Fire within me, light the garden cauldrons for our celebration. Help us embrace the fire of the sun and bring back the light of the moon. By the sweep of my hand, light the flames as I command."

With one swish of her wrist, the flame ignited in the cauldron before her. Subsequently, each of the smaller cauldrons around the garden also lit with their own flames. Autumn gave the fire a quick head nod in approval before Simone walked up beside her with a large silver pitcher of water.

"Ready?" Simone bent down with the pitcher. Autumn gave her the go-ahead, and Simone poured a continuous flow of water around the outer channel of the cauldron. The water flowed brilliantly in the light of the flames and rippled with golden shimmers.

"Perfect." Autumn turned to watch Aunt Jo pushing through the back door of the house carrying a massive pitcher of strawberry lemonade and a tray of cherry-red tomatoes dotted with green basil leaves and mozzarella cheese. "Oh, Aunt Jo! Let me help you with that."

"Thank you, dear!" Jo peered between her full hands as Tavish darted through her legs. "Tavish appears more excited than the rest of us for this evening! Although, if he makes me drop these dishes, he's not getting any salmon treats for a week!"

Autumn laughed as she took the large pitcher and poured drinks for each place at the wooden garden table. "Well, I'll give him more than enough treats for helping us out of this latest jam at the hot springs."

Jo smoothed her apron over her hips. "You're right. He's always around when you need him most, which is what a familiar worth his salt does."

"Hey, everyone!" Eve's voice called from around the side porch. "Lainy and I are here!" She walked around the side of the porch to the back garden carrying a large bag from the Forest Brew. "I come bearing gifts from my mother." She handed the bag to Jo, who immediately peeked inside and gasped.

"Oh, Catherine takes such good care of us!" Jo pulled out a basket carrying a gray linen tea towel bundled inside. She carefully unwrapped it to find still-steaming corn bread muffins heaped to the edge. "Wonderful! I have some local honey from Mrs. Pendleton, or I should say Freya, in the kitchen. I'll grab that for us as well."

"And Lainy's got the strawberry shortcake I made, too." Eve turned to look for Lainy behind her but didn't see her on the porch. "Uh, Lainy?"

"Yeah, I'm coming!" Lainy kicked off her expensive slide sandals as she came around the side of the porch with her arms full. "Sorry, somehow I attracted a couple fire ants to my feet, but I drew them to a bit of warmth, and they found their way." She walked to the large wooden table and set a champagne bottle in the center. "That's for later." Then, she set down a cake tray with a layered strawberry shortcake poised perfectly on top. "It'll go nicely with Eve's cake."

Penny wandered out the back door with a few yellow tapered beeswax candles and smiled brightly at the sight of everyone in the garden. "Oh, it's so lovely back here!" She placed the candles in the center of the table and waved Lainy and Autumn forward. "Girls, light the candles for us, please."

Lainy got started, and Autumn joined her. As they worked through each of the candles, Lainy felt it the right time to bring up last night.

"Autumn, about the book." Lainy blew out her fingertips as the last candle lit.

Shaking her head, Autumn sat down at the table. "I wanna talk to everyone about the Book of Spells, actually." She cleared her throat as they all settled into their chairs. "I know the MacKinnon Book of Spells was an ancestral heirloom for our family and our coven. While I'm deeply sorry I destroyed that part of our history, I know it was the right thing to do."

Penny reached across the table and grabbed her daughter's hand. "We know that was hard for you to do, dear."

"I want you to know that it won't go without purpose." Autumn looked around the table at each one of them. "The coven has a future that far exceeds the ways delineated within the spell book. It's up to us to set a new tone for our elemental magic going forward."

Eve perked up and smiled. "Oh, a new tone! We can learn from the old ways but create our path anew."

Simone chimed in. "I like where you're going with this. No course, just unchartered waters and the horizon stretched out in front of us."

"Like the sun rises, so, too, shall our Hollow's Glenn coven!" Lainy raised a glass of lemonade, and they all followed suit.

"To our Hollow's Glenn coven!" They toasted with uplifted energy.

"Rising with the sun . . . and the moon." Simone raised a finger to correct the toast.

"Oh!" Jo pushed her chair back from the table and went to the outer sill on the kitchen window. She grabbed the tarot card deck she had placed there earlier and returned. "That reminds me. I'd like to pull a card to read the energy for the upcoming season."

Tavish jumped up onto Jo's chair and sat patiently, eyeing Jo as she shuffled the deck. The cards flew between her fingers, and shimmers of turquoise and cobalt blue sprang from the deck as a card dropped to the table in front of her.

"There we go. Let's see." Jo flipped the card face up and studied it for a moment before showing the others. "Ah, yes." She turned the card around to reveal the familiar depiction of a crowned man riding in a carriage with two sphinxes below him. "The chariot. A powerful reminder that we have the ability to choose our course, but spirit remains with us the whole time." She nodded and glanced at the card once again, tapping on it with her finger. "This card tells me challenges lie ahead, but with confidence and strength, we can handle it all."

Autumn focused on the stars atop the crowned man on the card. She felt the ancestors' presence with them tonight, and she knew they would never leave her side.

Simone watched her cousin considering the card and interjected. "The different-colored sphinxes represent the duality and how we can flow with life and with the various aspects of ourselves. The light and the dark. The mind and the heart."

"Mmm, yes." Aunt Jo nodded along with her daughter and then glanced at Autumn, sensing what she had been feeling. "The many worlds that make up our inner and outer being. We must harness them all on the journey ahead."

Tavish put his paws on the table to inspect the card Jo had laid down. With a meow, he jumped down and ran to the back door of the house. Autumn watched him curiously and realized he wanted her to go inside.

Autumn stood from the table. "Excuse me for a second. I think Tav needs something inside, and I'll bring more lemonade out when I come back."

"Let me help you." Simone stood as well. "There's something I wanna give you." She threw her linen napkin down on the chair and walked into the house with Autumn. Quickly heading to the front entryway, Simone unlatched a small wooden door underneath the stairs. The hinge squeaked when she pulled it open to reveal a dark little closet full of peculiar items Aunt Jo kept.

Autumn sat on the hall bench beside the cupboard and waited as Simone pulled out a canvas covered in a drop cloth. As Simone removed the cover, Autumn's mouth dropped open. "Sim, what is this?"

Simone held the painting up under the light of the entry lantern. "I wanted to capture the silent power and connection you have now to the elements." She shrugged. "To show you all that's within you . . . and without."

The dark blues and eggplant tones blurred together on the canvas and shimmered with light in the entry. A woman with flowing auburn hair stood with her back to the viewer, a white owl perched on her right shoulder as she peered into the distance. In front of her sat the deep, saturated hues of a mountainous evergreen forest and the flowing river at its base. Over the trees, a hint of tangerine orange burst through the greens, showing dispersing rays of light.

Autumn stared at the painting in awe of its incredible magic. "It's . . . It's . . ." Trying to find the words, she shook her head back and forth.

"Do you like it?" Simone cringed for a minute. "I can't really tell from your aura right now."

Autumn beamed up at her cousin and stood to give her a warm hug. "It's the best gift you've ever given me, apart from always being by my side." She poured over every detail of the painting and pointed to the rays of light. "Is the sun supposed to be rising or setting?"

Simone smirked and drew her attention to that spot on the image. "Rising, setting . . . That's for you to decide. Either way, it's all within you."

The doorbell chimed suddenly and startled the girls out of their moment. They looked at each other in surprise, and both stopped to get a read on who it may be.

"Who in the world is coming over on the solstice?" Simone placed the painting carefully back under the stairs and closed the cupboard.

When she had it tucked neatly away, Autumn went to the oversized front door and tapped into her knowing.

Simone gave her cousin a look. "Someone's got a frustrated energy on the other side of that door. Let me grab a selenite crystal from the sitting room."

As her cousin disappeared into the next room, Autumn centered herself with a breath and opened the door. "Mrs. Halpin?" Autumn squinted at the brown-haired woman dressed in a lovely sun dress and pearls around her neck. "Is everything okay?"

Mrs. Halpin ran her fingers over her pearl necklace and kept glancing over at her left side. "Hello, Autumn. I'm so sorry to interrupt your summer solstice festivities this evening, but, well . . . I just can't take these visits anymore, and Stephen thought you'd be able to help."

Simone stepped beside Autumn at the door, holding a long stick of white selenite crystal at her side for cleansing. "Hello, Mrs. Halpin." Simone smiled at her and then immediately brought her attention over to the strange figure of a young man standing beside her. "Uh, I know as the mayor's wife, you're always lending a helping hand to those in need, but . . ." Simone pointed the selenite stick at the strange figure beside Mrs. Halpin. "Who's the ghost?"

Next In Series

Get the next book in the Hollow's Glenn Coven Mystery Series!

A Precipice of Envy, book 5 in the series, is available at the link below.

When a ghost returns from the grave to haunt the mayor's wife, the coven must determine whether his death truly was accidental. As the coven pulls together dormant clues, they discover a dark, sympathetic magic none of them wants to touch. Will the coven conquer their fears and uncover the reality of what happened to finally put this ghost to rest?

Don't miss another mesmerizing story with your favorite characters from Hollow's Glenn! Grab your copy now!
https://kristenkingwrites.com/hollowsglennseries

A Note From The Author

Thank you so much for reading my cozy paranormal mystery, *An Inferno of Ire.* I hope the characters spoke to you and that you fell in love with the inviting mountain town of Hollow's Glenn. If you'd like to share the enjoyment with fellow readers, then leaving an online book review would support those interested in cozy reads as well. That way, we can create a movement of magical readers in love with the worlds and possibilities in each story.

Now, as this book is part of the Hollow's Glenn coven mystery series, there will be more opportunities to get immersed in the world of the MacKinnon girls and the founding families. Plus, with each book, I'll share some practical magic such as Gran's tea recipes, Autumn's seasonal journaling prompts, and Eve's pastry recipes.

You can also hop onto my newsletter list to get the prequel with Penny's story of how she left for the mountain region and why she stayed so long. You may even find out how Autumn's gifts started.

To read the free prequel novella, *A Land of Consequence*, and hear about the latest releases and other goodies, go to:

https://dl.bookfunnel.com/azstlfr1se

Acknowledgments

To the beautiful island of Hawaii with its fire magic and elemental pull. Your energy captivated me from the moment I walked onto your lava rocks and felt the breezes moving onto the shoreline. I'll forever be grateful for experiencing your volcanoes, your waterfalls, your sunsets, your portal stones, your wildlife, and of course, your kind inhabitants. May your energy forever be a part of this earth and a part of my soul. Mahalo.

About The Author

Kristen is an Amazon best-selling author, life coach, and creative. After years of project management, design, and coaching, she now lets her water energy lead the way through creative fiction writing. She finds that a good dose of magic sets the coziest tone for any day.

When not channeling her inner writing muse, Kristen enjoys baking, snapping photos of her own mountain region, and practicing QiGong. She spends evenings snuggled next to a cozy fire with her family and calico cat, with plenty of candles and jazz playing softly in the background. Depending on the moon phase, you'll also find her pulling tarot cards or charging crystals by the light of the moon.

For more from the author and to find her books and offerings, go to:

https://www.kristenkingwrites.com